More Than Halfway There

More Than Halfway There

JANET HALLIDAY ERVIN

ILLUSTRATED BY TED LEWIN

FOLLETT PUBLISHING COMPANY

CHICAGO

Library of Congress Catalog Card Number: 77-118962

ISBN 0-695-40159-9 Titan binding
ISBN 0-695-80159-7 Trade binding

First printing I

737423

TO HOOSIER GRANDFATHERS LIKE MINE

Thanks to Frances Balcken, children's librarian, Wauwatosa (Wis.) Public Library, for her kindness and help.

The prayer on page 22 is adapted from a prayer that appeared in the *Indiana History Bulletin*: "The Indian Doctor," published by the Indiana Historical Bureau, March, 1964.

More Than Halfway There

1

It was a hazy October morning more than one hundred years ago. A boy with a gun trudged silently behind his father along a russet path through a woods in southern Indiana. The two had been walking since sunup. They were on their way to the nearest crossroads store at Gentryville where, they had been told, they could find a man who knew how to read.

The forest had been touched lightly with early frost. Now the sycamores and beeches, the tulip trees and redbud were garbed in autumn's carnival colors—wine, scarlet, and gold. On either side of the narrow footpath the crimson sumac flamed above masses of goldenrod and purple blazing-star. Against this background, the travelers struck a poor note in their homespun shirts, buckskin breeches, and battered wheat-straw hats.

The boy was not aware of fall's bright beauty. He had more important things to think about. For a long time he and his father had walked into the sunrise without speaking. Each carried a worry too big to talk about. The boy sensed the man's troubled spirit and, for the moment, was more bothered by it than by his own problem. He spoke out, hoping to cheer his father.

"I reckon I better be sighting me something to shoot. Likely it will be too dark by the time we start home."

He raised his gun to his shoulder and peered expertly along the barrel.

Lost in his own thoughts, the man didn't answer.

The boy, whose name was Albert Long, the same as his father, took careful aim. His finger curled around the trigger, but instead of firing, he dropped the gun to his side with a sound of disgust.

"Just a squirrel! I'm getting a mite tired of squirrel soup, ain't you, Pa?"

Mr. Long didn't stop walking. He only turned

his head and looked back at his son, a frown on his weathered face.

"Easy to get tired of something when it's plentiful," he said sharply. "I wager you'll be playing a different tune on your fiddle next winter. Come a snow like last year, we ain't likely to see fresh meat, squirrel or otherwise, till spring."

Albert thought back to the awful, pinching winter of 1828. No meat, little meal, and less money. But plenty of fever all through that part of Indiana. Luckily the Long family, even the newest baby, had come through it, though near neighbors had died.

This year they would try to be better situated, his father had said. They would lay by more salt-meat and cornmeal, apples and root vegetables, and medicine herbs—calomel, lobelia and cherryroot bark—to fight the fever. This year, praise the Lord, they would have some cash. If all went well in Gentryville, the paper which was poking up from his father's pocket would be converted into money. All the dollars that were left after buying supplies would be put into a little leather bag, and the bag tucked up behind the chimneypiece. If all went well in Gentryville . . .

"You don't want squirrel, so don't take it," Pa was going on more placidly. "You can afford to be choicey this time of year. Keep your eye peeled for partridge or turkey. Maybe you'll happen on a nice, fat doe."

Or a bear. Or an Indian. Albert moved his head from side to side, searching the bush. Deep in the woods in autumn, amid the blazing sumac, he could narrow his eyes and see a red man any time he wanted to. There was one now, the varmint—crouched in the brush, war paint gleaming on his naked brown body, white scalps dangling from his breechcloth, tomahawk lifted. Swiftly Albert raised his gun and plugged the savage right between his wicked eyes. How folks would talk from Pokeberry Creek to Pigeon River about brave, straight-shooting Albert Long.

His father jerked his head around. "Quit wastin' shot," he ordered.

"Yes, Pa." Albert opened his eyes wide, and the image of the Indian went away as it always did when Pa was along.

Anyway, he knew there were no bad Indians in these parts. It had been fifteen years since the last attack on white settlers. Other troubles had taken their place. Now, trouble could be a piece of paper. It could be an idea in a boy's head. Trouble could be a man.

"Pa—"

"What is it?"

"Suppose, when we get to Gentry's store, the reading man ain't there?"

"If he ain't, he ain't."

"How'll you get the paper witnessed?"

"Guess I won't. It don't have to be."

"What does the paper say again?"

Mr. Long grunted impatiently. "You know as well as me. It's an agreement between me and Peabody that I'll sell him some land."

"For one hundred dollars?"

"Yep."

"That's a heap of money, ain't it?"

His father sighed. "It's a right smart price, but I wish I didn't have to sell none of my land. I wouldn't neither if crops hadn't been so poor this year."

Albert wrinkled his forehead. "This is what I don't hardly understand—if you know what the paper says and Peabody knows, how come we have to go clear to town with it?"

Mr. Long touched the paper as if for luck. "I know what it's supposed to say. But when you make a bargain with a fellow, you want to make sure everything is straight. This man at Gentry's store will read it to me, then I'll sign it."

Albert's ears perked up. "Sign it? Can I watch?"

"No, you can't watch," his father mimicked.

15

"Land, but you're getting nibby as a coon. Now when we get to the store, you just tend to the supplies your ma ordered, and let me take care of men's business."

Albert had to know one more thing.

"How come you didn't sign the paper at home the way Peabody wanted you to?" he asked softly. "Don't you trust him?"

Mr. Long didn't answer, and Albert thought he had asked one question too many. Finally his father said quietly, "I wouldn't say I don't trust him, but he's new in these parts and he's rich and he's got some education, and you got to be careful of such fellows. Learning can put queer notions into a person. You don't hardly know what a man's thinking when he gets his ideas out of books."

His voice was lower and more troubled. "Yesterday, when I was out hunting, a dog crossed my path and, just after dawn, a flock of pigeons flew low past me. Some folks say these are bad luck signs."

Albert's eyes grew big. He had heard old grannies say such. Before he had time to reflect on the meanings of the dark omens, there was a whir of wings nearby and a blur of color swept up from the tall grass and disappeared into the woods.

"There!" his father grumbled. "A nice pair of

turkeys, and you could have had one easy if you hadn't been so busy nibbing into affairs that don't concern you. Will you hush now and start looking for us some supper?"

Albert was through asking questions. He had learned what he wanted to know.

I allowed that was it, he told himself.

Pa didn't trust Peabody. It wasn't just that the stranger was rich, but he could read and write. Pa couldn't do either, and this made him uneasy about business matters. It seemed to Albert that the conversation had worked itself around to the right place. This was the time to bring up the subject that had been on his mind for days. He stooped and picked up a buckeye and sailed it off through the red woods, trying to think how to begin. Best to jump right in. First though, for good luck, he rubbed the rabbit's foot in his pocket.

"Pa—" he took a deep breath, "I heard some news the other day."

"Well, what was it?"

Albert tried to keep his voice calm, not to let on that it mattered much.

"There's a new schoolmaster come to these parts."

"That so?" Pa's voice was cool.

"Yessir. Joe Hall told me. The schoolman

came all the way from Pennsylvany, and if there's enough pupils, he might settle here and not move on after winter like the rest."

Mr. Long shrugged. "I suppose he's got a right to settle if he's got two dollars for an acre."

"He's going to keep school in the cabin where we used to hold church whenever a preacher come by. That ain't hardly more than two-mile from our place. Why, a boy could walk that, even in snow, and be back and you'd hardly know he'd been gone."

Mr. Long opened his mouth to speak, but Albert pretended not to notice and plunged on.

"I been thinking, Pa, this here trip to Gentryville is a lot of bother for you. Wouldn't it be handy if we had someone, among our own kin, who could read and write and witness and such?" He rushed on, knowing he had used up his turn to speak, "I feel I could learn to do such, and I would pay the teacher myself with meat and skins so you wouldn't be out nothing." He stopped, then added pleadingly, "Can I go to school?"

Mr. Long had listened to this outburst thoughtfully, and his face, already clouded with worry over his own problem, grew darker. Abruptly he turned and seized Albert by the shoulder. As he looked down into his son's face, his expression changed from anger to disappointment.

18

"You've had your say," he began slowly, "now I'll have mine." He struggled for patience. "I ain't going to whip you, though I expect I should. At your age a boy is bound to get notions. I don't know where you're getting them, but I want to settle them once and for all.

"You'll recollect we spoke of this matter before, when the other schoolmaster came. I told you then, and I tell you now—there ain't nothing to schooling. If there was, don't you think I'd taken it up myself long ago?"

Sullenly Albert turned his head away. "The Grigsbys are going and the Jones kids and even Joe Hall."

He hated for Joe Hall to get ahead of him the way Mr. Hall had gone ahead of Pa. Mrs. Hall could read some, and both of them could sign their names. Joe was always bragging about it. The Halls' place was considerably finer than the Longs', even though Pa seemed to work harder than Mr. Hall. Albert wasn't sure, but he had always wondered if book learning had something to do with it.

"Let them all go to school," his father said sharply. "And while they're wasting the Lord's good time, you'll be learning to do a man's work." His voice took on a patient, pleading tone. "What does it take to be a man? You got to be able to shoot straight, clear your land and work it, build yourself a cabin, butcher, plow, plant, harvest. There's no end to the work if you're going to keep a roof over your head and food in your mouth. It's root-hog-or-starve in this world, Albert.

"Reading and writing. How often does a person need them? Like this paper—I take it to a fellow that can fix it up and then I go back to useful work. As for the reading man at Gentry's—I don't know him at all, but I don't have much use for him. A fine-haired creature who sets and reads to folks. I wager he don't own no land. He ain't worth a hill of beans, would you say?"

It was a long speech for Pa, and he wasn't through. Before Albert could answer, his argument took a new turn.

"Anyway, what makes you think you got a head for learning? Why, I knew a fellow once that went to school three or four months, and he didn't get much out of it. You're a good hand to work, same as me, but I never figured I'd be any great shakes at books and I don't see none of it in you neither."

"I'm as smart as Joe Hall," Albert said stubbornly. "If he can learn, I can, too."

"No, you can't," his father said, " 'cause you ain't gonna waste time trying. Let's hear no more of it. Hustle along—no, wait—shh!"

He nudged his son and pointed straight ahead. They both stopped and stood very still. Slowly

20

Albert raised his gun. He took careful aim at the distant tree, then gently squeezed the trigger. There was a thud in the grass ahead. A flurry of feathers floated down from the hawthorne tree and settled in the leaves, as the shot echoed from the woods.

"You got her!" Mr. Long plunged ahead into the bushes. "A pretty shot—a mighty pretty shot." He strode back, swinging the turkey by its neck. "I don't believe your cousin Hiram could have done better."

Albert couldn't keep from grinning. That was high praise for sure. His father thought a lot of Hiram, who was known as one of the best shots in those parts.

"Imagine a boy who can shoot like that wanting to ruin his eyes on books," Mr. Long scoffed. "Here, take your bird. Your ma will be pleased to see it."

Single file, they resumed their journey. Albert wasn't as disappointed as he had expected to be. After all, he really hadn't had much hope of changing his father's mind about school. They had discussed the matter before, and now it was settled for good. Pa's praise of his marksmanship rang pleasantly in his ears. It was a rare thing for his father to hand out compliments.

He studied the tall figure striding ahead of him

—the muscular shoulders and sinewy arms, the strong brown hands, hard and gnarled as a hickory root. Those hands could split a log or plow a furrow faster and straighter than most any man's around. If Pa said schooling wasn't much account, likely it was so.

Where did I pick up such fool ideas anyway? Albert wondered.

Was it that gray December day two years back when his grandma died of the fever? The doctor couldn't save her and none of the herbs and roots known to the Indians—heart's ease, calomel, sassafras, bloodroot, rattlesnake gall, slippery elm, nanny tea, or sulphur—helped her. They prayed to the day as the old grannies advised by gathering around the sick woman's bed, saying together:

"Good morning, dear Monday. Take away from Grandma the seventy-seven-fold fevers. Oh . . . take them away from her!"

But nothing helped.

They held the burying without a preacher, because none came around till the following spring. As they smoothed the frozen clods of yellow clay over the fresh grave, his mother cried, "I'd feel better if somebody could read the Bible."

The Longs owned a Bible that Mrs. Long brought from Virginia as a bride, but they knew no one who could make it out except Joe Hall's folks, and Pa wouldn't stand for asking them.

"Someday I'll learn," Albert had whispered to comfort her, "and I'll read it to you anytime you want."

His mother had smiled at him. "I'll be proud to listen." There was doubt in her eyes, but she squeezed his hand for the thought.

Nothing more was ever said about it, so it was strange that the memory had stayed with him as a promise that ought to be kept. Over the past two years Albert's daydreams had grown bigger. If a person could learn to read the Bible, couldn't he learn to read doctor books, too, and maybe discover a cure for the fevers and chills that plagued folks the year around?

Looking back to those days and dreams, Albert wished he had been born educated. Looking at his father, he wished he had never heard of reading and writing. He didn't know exactly what he wished; he was all mixed-up. If only he had the gumption of his cousin Hiram. Hiram was sixteen and he was never mixed-up. He knew just what he wanted.

"You'd never catch me in school!" Hiram exclaimed when he heard a new teacher was coming. "I'd rather hunt and fish. Why, I'd rather shuck corn and hoe weeds than set there studyin'. What good is it? Does it put food on the table? Does it put dollars in your pocket? Why, I wouldn't go to school even if my pa would let me."

In a way, it was a good thing Hiram felt that way about school. Good for the schoolmaster, anyway. Albert's cousin could be a roughneck when he pleased, and unless the teacher was pretty big and fast with a beech switch, Hiram and his friends were liable to pitch him right into the creek to show him who was boss.

Anyway, Albert concluded, his cousin showed good sense about book learning. That was the best way to feel about something that was beyond you.

"Don't pout." Mr. Long caught sight of his son's serious expression. "If there's anything I can't abide, it's a pith-mouth. There's no call for you to be long faced today." He talked over his shoulder as he strode along.

"We're rich folks, don't you know? This here paper in my pocket is as good as cash. We're going to save some, but we're going to spend some, too. Not just for regular supplies either but for extras— some white sugar for your ma, as well as brown and some sorghum and maple syrup and, maybe, some new dishes."

Albert listened, openmouthed. He had never heard his father talk so recklessly.

24

"And some kind of pretty for your little sisters like a dolly with a painted face maybe, if they ain't too dear, and what would you say," his father looked at him slyly, "to boots?"

"Boots!" Albert gasped. "For me?" He had never had a pair of store-bought shoes, much less real boots, though he had admired Joe Hall's many a time.

"We've scraped along poor," his father said gruffly. "Now we're going to be rich till it gives out."

His smile at his son's excitement did not conceal the anxious note in his voice.

Should we spend our money on such fine goods? Albert wondered uneasily. When our land is gone and the money, too, what then? He decided not to worry about it. If Pa said it was all right, it must be.

He heard a man say once, "I been poor, and I been rich, and rich is better." He knew it was true. Rich was better than anything. It made you feel different inside, warm, comfortable, safe. Education didn't hold a candle to it. He saw it plainly. A man didn't get prosperous by reading books but by working hard with his hands.

"Hey, Pa—" He trotted to catch up with his father. "Forget what I said about school, will you? I wouldn't give you two cents for it."

2

The two walkers hadn't reached the edge of the woods when they began to hear voices, shouts, and laughter. Grinning at each other, they quickened their steps and soon came into the clearing which was the village of Gentryville. Albert stopped and stared.

"Looky here," he whistled in surprise. "Folks as thick as bees aswarming."

Mr. Long seemed just as pleased to be in town where things were humming. "I reckon they're waiting for the wagons to bring up the supplies from Rockport and Troy where the boats come in."

They stopped to rest under a large tulip tree where they could observe the crowd and perhaps spy an acquaintance.

"Where do the boats come from, Pa?" Albert had heard his father's river stories many times, but he was always ready to listen again. The names of faraway places, called out one after the other, were like a song. Each time they were told, the boy felt that he had been away on a journey and had come home again.

"Oh, they come from Pittsburgh and Baltimore to the east, and from Evansville to the west, down the Wabash River from Terry Hut and Vincennes, and up the Mississippi and Ohio from New Orleans and Natchez."

"What do they bring from that far?"

"Sugar, rice, cotton, tobaccy, and fancy things, fruit, jewelry, perfume, fine dress goods, for them as can afford it."

"Like us," Albert said happily. "You've been around the river a lot, ain't you, Pa?" Albert urged the story along.

"Oh, quite a bit. When I lived on the Kentucky side of the Ohio River, before your time, I used to watch the boats every day. It's a great sight. That's why it gets my goat when they talk of raising taxes to build roads and canals and railroads. Ain't nothing in this country ever going to take the place of the river for travel and transport."

Albert listened respectfully, marvelling at his father's knowledge of the world.

"I swan! If it ain't the Albert Longs, father and son."

Mr. Long had been stretched out on the ground, resting. Now he jumped to his feet. "Hoggy Jenks! Glad to see you."

The short plump man shook hands heartily, his round face pink with pleasure.

"Hey there, boy," he reached over and rumpled Albert's hair.

"How's your copperosity?"

"Doing fine, Mr. Jenks," Albert grinned.

The question always tickled him. He didn't know what your "copperosity" was; it was just something folks said, meaning, "How's your health?"

Albert had always liked Mr. Jenks, who was called Hoggy by his friends. The name fit because he was about an axe-handle wide and, with his round, red face and fat belly bulging over his rope belt, looked like a plump little shoat.

The Jenkses had first settled on Pokeberry Creek near the Longs, but their land played out and they moved on down Pigeon River. Now he caught sight of the hen turkey lying at the foot of the tulip tree.

"That's a whopper!" he said admiringly to Mr. Long. "You bring her down?"

Mr. Long jerked his thumb toward Albert.

Jenks beamed. "I always did say he was the likeliest young'un in this neck of the woods."

"Oh, he's all right when he's asleep," Albert's father sounded modest but looked proud. "He'll do fine if he can keep his mind off foolishness."

Jenks shifted his cud of tobacco to the other cheek and spat a long brown stream which barely missed Albert's foot.

"Your family well?"

"Tolerable since we got over the fever," Mr. Long answered. "How about you folks?"

"Pretty good," Jenks nodded. "Though my missus did have the hives real bad from eating love apples. I warned her, but she wouldn't listen. Broke all out. 'Call 'em tomateys or whatever you please,' I says to her. 'Them things may look pretty in the garden, but they're poison as all get-out.' She wanted me to try 'em, but I says, 'No, I ain't that anxious to make you a widow.' Women folks." He shook his head in disgust. "You can't tell 'em nothing."

"How's your sister and husband?" Mr. Long asked. "The ones that moved up to Illinois last year."

Jenks's smile faded. "That's what brings me here." He pulled a letter from the pocket of his jeans. "My sister has been real poorly. I got this letter from her husband four, five days ago. Been trying to find time to get into town and get it read. If she ain't better, I'm going up for a visit. She's the only kin I got left, you know."

Mr. Long expressed his sympathy, saying that his wife always thought a lot of Jenks' sister. "I hope it's good news you have there."

"I trust it is. By the way, what brings you to town today?"

Mr. Long cleared his throat. "Oh, something of the kind."

"A letter?" Jenks looked curious.

"No, not a letter. Just a business paper I want witnessed."

"Not selling out, are you?"

"Nothing like that."

Albert could see that his father didn't want to discuss the matter, even with a friend.

"I'm just selling a little piece of my land. Hate to do it, but crops was so poor this year. I'm mighty short of cash."

"You and me and everybody," Jenks said

mournfully. "Remember what high hopes we had when we came here in 1816?" He turned to Albert. "That was the year Indiana came into the Union free, the year we called eighteen-hundred-and-froze-to-death. It was a terrible, bad winter . . . frost in the fields till May . . . hay went to a hundred dollars a ton . . ."

The two men began to reminisce about the old days, and how hard they had worked to clear the land. Hoggy sighed as if the memory of all that hard work tired him.

"Once we got it cleared though, it was awful nice fertile soil. Crops was good those first years, except in '22 when the gray squirrels ate all the corn and in '26 when the armyworms got into the wheat and rye. But now it appears that the soil is about worked out." He looked sharply at Mr. Long. "Who you selling your piece of land to?"

Albert's father hesitated. "Henry Peabody."

"Peabody!" Hoggy Jenks gave a low whistle. "Watch Peabody. He didn't get rich looking out for other folks' health."

Albert glanced anxiously at his father.

"I ain't worried," said Mr. Long. But he looked worried.

"I am itching to get shut of the deal though. Come on, son, let's go into the store and get this matter tended to."

"Whoa—" Hoggy held up a hand. "I 'spect you'll have to get in line. Every man here has something he wants read or writ or witnessed."

Mr. Long was surprised to hear it.

"Yep. Old man Gentry was complaining about it last time I was in. 'If you folks don't stop taking up my clerk's time reading,' Gentry says, 'I'm gonna start charging for the service.'" Hoggy chuckled. "He won't though. He knows it's good for business. It gets people into the store, and once they hear the newspapers read, it gives them ideas of more things to buy."

"Who is the reading man anyway?" Mr. Long asked. "A schoolteacher come out from the East?"

Hoggy shook his head. "Nope. He ain't one of your fine-haired Yankees. He's one of us from right here in Pigeon Creek. Yet he ain't one of us neither. He's different. His cousin Dennis Hanks, said just the other day that there's something peculiarsome about him."

"I don't care how peculiarsome he is," said Mr. Long, "if he can just make out this here paper."

Hoggy Jenks declared that he had never seen anything yet that could stump the fellow. He was awful smart and real likeable, too. Told the funniest stories you ever heard. Children took to him. He'd play marbles with them, run footraces, wrestle, and tell them stories.

32

Albert looked interested, but his father observed that children generally did like loafers.

"Oh, he ain't idle," Jenks protested. "If only you can keep him away from books. He can husk two loads of corn to another man's one. He can sink an axe deeper into wood than any fellow you ever saw. Why, if you heard him felling trees, you'd swear there was three men at work. But if he comes across something to read, look out. Pretty soon you'll see him laid up against a tree somewheres, lost to the world in his book and the corn just waiting."

The two broke into laughter at the idea of a grown man reading while work waited.

Suddenly their conversation was interrupted by a terrible commotion. Two rough-looking men who had been arguing on the porch of the store started to fight. Hot-eyed, they circled round and round each other like two strange tomcats, poking, jabbing, kicking. One grabbed the other and wrestled him to the ground. Over they rolled, tussling and pounding and swearing, while the onlookers formed a circle around them, enjoying the entertainment.

"One of them wild Corey boys is mixing it up with a riverman," Hoggy Jenks said disapprovingly. "I don't know which one's the worst. Listen to that language. Both full of whiskey, like as not." He turned to Albert. "Stay away from the river, boy."

Mr. Long agreed with him that the flatboatmen were a rough bunch.

"You got to watch the company you keep," he warned. "If you lay down with dogs, you're gonna get up with fleas."

"Oh, don't worry about this boy," Jenks said confidently. "He comes from good stock. Apples don't fall far from the tree, you know."

Albert knew he meant that children usually turn out to be pretty much like their parents. It suited him to hear it, since he already had decided that he was going to try to be just like his father.

The fight seemed to be over. Friends had separated the two scrappers who stood panting and glaring at each other. Bored with adult conversation, Albert wandered away toward the pasture behind the store where a group of boys were playing Four Corner Bullpen. As Albert arrived, they switched to a game of Tag. Sure enough, there was Joe Hall in the thick of it.

"Hey, Joe!"

Albert was glad to see him. Joe wasn't a bad kid when he wasn't blowing and bragging. Anyway, Albert didn't get many chances to play with boys his own age. Joe waved and beckoned him to get into the game. Albert lost no time. Being fast on his feet, he managed to dodge around, dart in and out and avoid being tagged by the oldest Grigsby boy who was "It." After several passes, Grigsby gave up trying to catch Albert and took out after Joe Hall. He tagged him easy as pie and Albert couldn't keep from grinning. If there was one thing Joe couldn't blow about, it was his running. He was too slow to catch cold. Joe saw the grin, and a sly look came over his face.

"Hey, Albert." He waved something shiny over his head. "You got one of these?"

Albert slowed down to take a better look. It was a new jackknife. He stared enviously.

"You're It!" Joe gave him a whack that was more than a tap. Scowling, Albert started after him, planning to trip him and send him sprawling for his smart-aleck ways. Suddenly he saw something that stopped him. Coming up the slope toward Gentry's store was the tallest man he had ever seen. He was probably 'way over six foot because his jeans didn't come anywhere near meeting his shoe tops but instead exposed a length of bare shanks. Albert looked up to the rugged face topped by unruly black hair. On each shoulder he carried a good-sized keg, and as he strode along he balanced the kegs as easily as newborn lambs. A closer look revealed hard knots of muscles bulging under his calico shirt —muscles you would hardly expect to see in such a slim fellow.

Albert punched Joe. "Who's that?"

Instead of answering, Joe gave a whoop and a holler like the rest of the boys and ran for the newcomer. Some jumped on his back, while others tackled him around the knees.

"Boys! Boys!" the tall young man pleaded. "Quit pestering me. I got work to do." But they clung to him all the tighter. "All right then," he gave in good-naturedly. "Let me get rid of these kegs."

No sooner had he set his burdens on the ground than they all ganged up on him and soon had him lying flat, though it took four of the biggest boys to hold him. Albert watched in delight. He would have liked to get into the tussle, but he didn't feel like acting so fresh with a stranger.

One of the boys who was straddling a knee called out, "This here is the longest leg I ever saw."

"That so?" The captive lifted his head to inspect the leg. "Well, here's another just like it." Catching them off guard, he kicked out his other leg, wrenched himself free and sprung to his feet.

The boys roared their approval at this show of strength. Albert thought it one of the cleverest tricks he had ever seen. He moved in closer, hoping

36

to meet the fellow, but there was no more horse-play. Someone in the crowd called out, "Give us a speech!" and the rest took up the cry.

Without further urging, the young man leaped onto a stump, and threw out his arms for silence.

"Friends, fellow Hoosiers," he began dramatically, "today I wish to speak to you on this subject: Who Has the Most Right to Complain—the Negro or the Indian?"

The boys grew quiet. The men stopped talking. Even the horse traders over by the hitching posts left off their haggling and drew in close to listen. The high, thin voice rose and fell on the autumn air as the speaker, waving his arms for emphasis, compared the troubles of the red man driven from his land with the plight of the black man held in slavery.

Albert, who had rejoined his father and Mr. Jenks, listened intently. He didn't understand all of it, but what he did understand sounded true. Both races had suffered at the hands of the white man. He had never thought about it before. The speaker concluded his argument with a little bow, but the crowd wouldn't let him go.

"Give us one of your pomes."

The speaker grinned, happy to be asked.

"I've recently committed a new poem to memory, and it's one of my favorites."

The smile faded from his face as he began solemnly:

Oh, why should the spirit of mortal be proud?
Like a swift-fleeting meteor, a fast-flying
cloud,
A flash of the lightning, a break of the wave,
He passeth from life to his rest in the
grave . . .

There were a great many other verses, all ending with, *Oh, why should the spirit of mortal be proud?*

The speaker bowed once more. "I thank you, friends, for your kind attention." He jumped down from the stump, shouldered his kegs, and marched into the store.

Hoggy Jenks slapped his knee. "You'd swear it was Governor Jim Ray hisself, wouldn't you? He can go on like that all day on about any subject."

"Who is that long drink of soup anyway?" Albert's father asked.

"Why, that's Gentry's clerk—the reading man."

"Sure ain't much to look at," Mr. Long grunted. "Plain as an old shoe."

"But strong as a bull," Albert added admiringly.

"And smart as paint," Jenks declared. "He

38

ain't but twenty years old, but he's the smartest feller in these parts. Some folks say he's smart enough to run for office. And to think he got it all out of books."

Mr. Long shrugged. "Books are all right, I suppose, if you got time for them, but too much studying tends to make the brain soft."

"That's what they say. I ain't sure about it though. Old coot as I am—" Jenks looked all around to make sure nobody else was listening, "it gives me a hankering to go to school whenever I listen to Abe Lincoln."

3

Boots! Glossy, brown, calfskin boots, smartly laced,
standing straight and proud as soldiers on the shelf.
Albert could almost reach across the counter and
touch them. And they were his, as much as if they
had his name on them. It occurred to him that
somebody else might buy them first, so he decided
to ask Mr. Gentry to set them aside until Pa had
the cash in hand. He looked around for the storekeeper and found both him and the clerk at the
far end of the store surrounded by customers. They
were too busy to be bothered by a boy.

Some of the men were helping themselves to

supplies, hefting huge sacks of flour or meal to their shoulders and carrying them outside to carts or wheelbarrows. Others were waiting for Mr. Gentry to measure out coffee, sugar, beans or rice. Those who had brought farm produce to barter, instead of money, were haggling over the worth of their products. Many had formed a line, as Hoggy Jenks had predicted, and were waiting for the clerk who already had taken his seat behind the counter and had begun to read a letter to the first man in line. Mr. Long and Hoggy Jenks were among those waiting.

Likely nobody else would buy the boots, Albert told himself. They had been standing in the same place the last time he came to Gentry's with Pa. That day, last spring, he had hung over the counter, staring at them longingly, never dreaming that one day they would belong to him. Not many folks could afford such luxury. Joe Hall's boots weren't half as fine. Just to make sure they would be safe, Albert sat down on a nail keg nearby to keep watch over them.

"Help yourself to a pickle." Mr. Gentry, hustling by with a jug of sorghum molasses in each hand, caught sight of Albert patiently waiting.

"Much obliged."

Staring down into the pickle barrel, he stuck in his hand and fished around until he found what appeared to be the biggest, fattest dill. Funny that old man Gentry should turn so soft all of a sudden. Usually he didn't hurt himself, giving stuff away. Likely he had heard about Pa's business deal and was looking forward to selling heaps of merchandise to the Longs, for cash this time.

Things sure were different when a person was rich. Albert settled down contentedly to suck the sour pickle, go over the staples his mother had ordered, and study the fancy goods on the shelves.

There had been times in the past when he almost hated to look at the bright, colorful objects, knowing they weren't for him. Today it was pure pleasure to run his eyes over the pretty calicoes, the china dishes and sparkling glassware, and the sturdy, ready-made tools. There were wooden pails of hard candy that some children received for Christmas. There was a china-headed doll with blue eyes and a white pinafore and bonnet. The only dolls his sisters had ever owned were made of corncobs and dressed in homespun garments sewn by his mother. There were mittens and moccasins, furs and hides, saddles and ox yokes. There was a shiny jackknife, bright enough to see your face in.

"What you doing?" Joe Hall inched an empty keg up close and sat down.

"Eating this pickle Mr. Gentry gave me free and watching my boots."

"What boots?"

42

Albert had a hard time hiding a grin at the look of astonishment on Joe's face.

"Go on. Your pa ain't buying you them boots."

"He is so and that jackknife, too, probably, and some of that pretty cloth for my ma, and some new tools and white sugar, and a doll for my sisters."

Albert knew he was talking bigger than he should, but he had listened to Joe Hall's bragging so often, he wanted to get even.

"Where's your list then?" Joe asked suspiciously. "Oh, excuse me," he laughed. "Now, my ma, when she wants something from the store, she *writes* her out a list. Then my pa brings it along and *reads* it to Gentry. That's what I'll be doing after I start school this winter. You're going to school, ain't you?"

Albert's face was growing hot right up to the tips of his ears.

"If your pa can read and write so good," he challenged Joe, "how come he's in line with the rest, waiting for the reading man?"

"Why, he just wants Abe Lincoln to witness his signature on a paper." Joe smiled as if it was the dumbest question in the world. "And when my father signs his name, he really signs it—he don't just make his mark like some folks' fathers. By the way, what's your pa doing up there? Did he find gold on your place, or what?"

"None of your business," Albert muttered.

"He ain't selling his land, is he?" Joe persisted shrewdly. "We heard Henry Peabody was going around, trying to buy up land cheap. My pa wouldn't have nothing to do with him."

Fed up with Joe's showing off, Albert turned to give him a shove, when suddenly both boys were roughly jostled and almost fell off their seats.

"Out of my way! Lemme through!" A coarse looking man elbowed his way through the crowd, pushing everyone aside. It was the same fellow who had picked a fight with the riverman. As he reeled past, he left a smell of whiskey trailing behind him.

There were cries for him to get in line and to take his turn, but he didn't pay any attention. Staggering up to the counter, ahead of the rest, he thrust a paper into the clerk's face.

"Read this to me," he commanded in a loud voice.

The clerk looked up. "Wait your turn, Jack."

The man leaned forward unsteadily. "I ain't got time to wait," he said in an ugly voice. "Read it now."

The clerk looked at him. "I'm not going to read it at all unless you calm down and wait your turn. You can't come in here full of whiskey, scratching like a wildcat."

The troublemaker was not as tall as the clerk, but he was heavier. He looked as if he was used to starting fights and winning them, too. He thrust his face close to the clerk.

"You think you're so smart with all your book learning, Abe Lincoln. Well, I'm as smart as you."

The clerk smiled. "Suppose you read the paper to me then."

"Watch out for trouble," a man nearby said in a low voice. "Abe don't hold with drinking."

In the excitement Albert and Joe Hall forgot their own feud. Chances looked good for another fight. Quickly they edged forward, moving up near Mr. Long and Mr. Jenks where they could get a better view.

The drinking man drew back his arm threateningly. The clerk spoke sharply to him. The man doubled his fist and swung. The clerk threw up a protecting hand and stepped backward.

"Come on and fight," sneered the bully, waving his fist.

Albert's father grinned at Jenks. "Looks like he's got your reading man buffaloed."

"Keep watching," Jenks drawled.

The clerk stretched out a long arm as if to ward off the next blow, then fast as lightning he twisted his hand around, and caught the bully by the back of his collar. With his other hand he took a firm grip on the seat of the man's jeans. Lifting him off the floor as easily as a sack of flour, he carried him through the crowd to the door and out into the yard. Across the lot he marched with his struggling captive to the horse trough. There he dumped him with a great splash. The man flailed and floundered around, cursing and spluttering.

The clerk dusted off his hands. "Come back when you can act civilized," he said sternly.

All the customers in Gentry's store had crowded to the doorway to watch. They roared with laughter and slapped the clerk on the back admiringly when he strolled back into the store. He took his place behind the counter.

"Anybody else want to fight before we get on with our reading?" he asked calmly.

Albert and Joe looked around hopefully, but to their disappointment, there were no takers.

"We won't see any more of that roughneck," Mr. Long predicted.

Hoggy Jenks chuckled. "Sure we will. He'll be back before long, dripping like an ash hopper but meek as a lamb. The wild boys around here learned long ago that Abe Lincoln is slow to get mad, but when he is riled, he can outfight 'em as well as outthink and outtalk 'em. But once in a while some bird forgets it and has to learn all over again. Well, looks like I'm next in line. Howdy, Abe."

"Howdy, Jenks."

They shook hands warmly as if they were old friends.

"What can I do for you?"

"Abe, I been carrying this letter around four, five days, trying to get in with it."

The clerk took the rumpled letter, smoothed it out before him and began to read silently. Presently he looked up at Jenks, his face solemn.

"I hate to have to read this to you."

Jenks looked anxious. "Ain't bad news, I hope. Has my sister taken a turn for the worse?"

"Your sister died a week ago today."

"No!" Jenks was shocked. "Why, I never thought—"

The clerk began to read the letter in a soft voice. From time to time, the plump man mopped his eyes with a huge red bandanna handkerchief. All the jolliness had gone from his round pink face. The clerk folded the letter and handed it back.

"I'm terribly sorry."

"Much obliged, Abe," Jenks said sadly. "I do wish I'd known sooner though. I might have got up to Illinois for the burying. To think I been carrying this bad news around in my pocket, never knowing." Sighing, he shuffled over to the rocking chair that stood by the potbellied stove. He sat down heavily and, to calm his nerves, pulled out a plug of tobacco and began to shave it with his pen-knife and cram the shavings into a corncob pipe.

"Next," the clerk called.

Mr. Long stepped forward and cleared his throat.

"My name is Albert Long. I come from up Pokeberry Creek way. I have a business paper here that I'd be obliged if you'd witness."

Albert moved closer to his father, and the clerk smiled at him as he reached for the paper. He read it over carefully.

"Yes. Everything seems to be in order, Mr. Long, and I see Mr. Peabody has already signed. Now you put your signature right here," he pointed to a line at the bottom of the paper, "and I'll witness the signing."

Mr. Long hesitated in embarrassment. The clerk seemed to understand.

"I see," he nodded pleasantly. "Just make your mark then, and I'll write your name for you."

After the clerk had signed, Mr. Long took the quill pen awkwardly in hand and leaned forward over the paper. Albert stood on tiptoe, peering over his father's shoulder to watch him draw the X. Pa still seemed uncertain.

"Would you kindly read me what the paper says?" he asked timidly.

48

"Gladly." The clerk began to read:

"I, Albert Long, agree to sell to Henry Peabody, for the sum of one hundred dollars, my entire farm with land, buildings and livestock."

Albert sucked in his breath. He felt as if he had been hit in the stomach with a rock. He looked up at his father who appeared to have been struck, too. Pa's face was as red as a rooster's comb; his mouth hung open dumbly.

"Sell my farm?" he repeated as if in a daze. "For one hundred dollars? My whole farm with house and animals? That ain't right. I was just aiming to sell him a piece of my land."

The clerk studied him gravely. "That isn't what this paper says."

Mr. Long's expression changed from bewilderment to anger. He shook his fist at the clerk, then brought it crashing down on the counter.

"It's a lie!" he shouted.

Albert was scared. He looked for the tall clerk to handle Pa the way he had handled the drinking man. But the clerk didn't seem to be mad at the shouting. He looked as if he felt sorry.

"It may be a lie, Mr. Long," he said quietly, "but it isn't my lie."

Hoggy Jenks spoke up mournfully from his seat near the stove. "Peabody will skin you every time." He stared into the fire. "Well, as the Good Book says, Man is born to trouble as the sparks fly upward."

"Can't trust nobody except Abe," hiccuped a voice.

It was the former troublemaker, who had sneaked back into the store and was drying out by the stove.

Noisy conversation broke out among the men as they discussed Henry Peabody's treachery. Some seemed worried that such a thing might happen to them. Others were amused by the trick, since it wasn't their ox that was gored. Mr. Long's color had faded from angry red to sick gray. He breathed heavily as if he was in need of fresh air.

"For your trouble," he said shortly, pushing a coin across the counter.

The clerk pushed it back. "No charge."

Mr. Long pushed it forward. "Take it!"

"No charge," the clerk repeated pleasantly but firmly.

Mr. Long glared at him for a moment, then stuck the money in his pocket, grabbed the paper, crumpled it in his hand and wheeled around to face Albert.

"I'm going down to the road with the men to watch for the wagons," he snapped. "You stay here and get the supplies."

50

It wasn't fair. Albert had looked forward to watching the wagons come up from Rockport, too. He would be the only one left behind. But he wouldn't give his father an argument right now. Pa had been made a fool of in front of people. It would be a good while before he got over it.

At the door, Mr. Long turned back.

"Don't get nothing but the necessities," he said gruffly.

Albert understood. They were poor folks again. No money. No boots. No dishes or dolls, white sugar or hard candy for Christmas. Mentally he prepared himself for another year of nothing. But Pa's promise of "rich" had been so sweet, it was hard not to feel cheated.

Joe Hall passed by with his father on his way to the road. There was a sorrowful look on his face.

"My, that's too bad, Albert," he said solemnly.

It was all Albert could do to keep from punching him. He knew Joe was laughing on the inside.

4

There was only the tick-tick of the old clock and the crackling of the fire in the stove to keep Albert company. The clerk was there, but he might as well have left with the rest. He was lost in his newspaper, not even aware of another's presence. A big, black cat with unfriendly yellow eyes and a nervous tail was curled in his lap.

Albert leaned in dejection against the counter, his gaze roaming listlessly about the silent room. Only a few minutes before, the bright objects which lined the shelves had appeared so exciting, so desirable. Now all had lost their luster.

Not yours, not yours, not yours, the old clock seemed to say.

In boredom Albert shifted his gaze to the face of the reading man, half wishing the fellow would come to and talk to him, yet not knowing what to say if he did. It was a face "plain as an old shoe," his father had said, yet full of strength. The clerk had a large head with thick, bushy, black hair, which he constantly rumpled with his fingers as he read, as if the action helped him think better. His skin was brown and leathery like most men who worked long hot hours in the Indiana cornfields. His gray eyes were deep-set under heavy eyebrows. His nose was large and his mouth wide and generous, and his ears stood out from his head as if they were seeking information. High cheekbones and a strong jaw gave him something of the look of an Indian. It was a wonder to watch the fellow read. Albert had known folks like Joe Hall's mother who could pick out words slowly, but never had he seen eyes move so swiftly across a printed page. His foot began to tingle from standing in one position. Quietly as possible, he scraped his moccasin back and forth on the puncheon floor. The reading man jerked his head up.

"I thought I was all by myself," he said in surprise. "Can I do something for you, son?"

Albert had been wrestling with an idea. He

didn't know whether he should go through with it. Impulsively he reached down and picked up his turkey by the neck.

"Here—" he thrust it out boldly. "I shot it myself."

"For me?" The clerk looked puzzled. "What have I done to deserve such a fine gift?"

"It's for keeping my pa from getting skinned."

Albert's face grew red at the memory of Pa's shame.

"Why, you don't owe me anything—" The clerk seemed to sense the boy's discomfort. "Well, if you want me to have this, I'll be proud to accept it."

A warm, friendly smile spread over the rough features and made them almost good-looking.

"My ma will be mighty tickled to see this nice hen. She keeps after me to bring home some game, but I'm not much hand for shooting. I am a great hand for eating turkey, though. I thank you."

He laid the bird carefully on a burlap sack on the floor beside him, then turned back to Albert.

"Can I help you to something in the store?"

Albert shook his head. He had decided to let his father buy the supplies. He wasn't sure now that they could afford anything unless Mr. Gentry gave them more credit. He might as well make up his mind to love squirrel soup. Looked as if he was going to be eating it the rest of his life. Of course, if there was a big snow and a long hard freeze on top of it, most of the squirrels would be frozen and starved out, and the few left would fall prey to the lean, gray wolves that would prowl closer and closer to the cabin.

"I'll just wait for my pa to come back."

"Might as well wait sitting down." The clerk pulled another chair close to the stove. "Want a piece of newspaper to look at?"

Albert shook his head again.

"Can't read?"

"Nope."

"Ever expect to learn?"

Albert wrinkled his nose as his cousin Hiram would have done, as if he didn't think much of the idea.

"My pa says it ain't worth much."

The clerk drew his bushy eyebrows together in a frown. "I'm sorry to have to disagree with a boy's pa."

Albert looked away uncomfortably. The matter of school had been settled for him. He didn't care to chew it over.

"What's your name, son?"

"Albert Long, same as my father."

"Mine's Abraham Lincoln—call me Abe." He leaned forward and gripped the boy's hand. "Howdy, Albert." He stared, wrinkling his forehead. "Albert Long—Abe Lincoln—I swan! You and I have the same initials."

Albert looked blank.

Abe said it again. "The same initials—A L—don't you see?"

Albert didn't see.

"Here, let me show you."

Shooing the black cat off his lap, he stretched out a long arm and took a pencil from a shelf. Stretching the other arm, he brought out a piece of brown wrapping paper from behind the counter. He did all this without rising an inch from his chair.

A wingspread like a turkey buzzard, Albert thought.

"Hitch up your chair here, watch close and I'll show you something mighty interesting."

After doubling the newspaper on his knee, Abe spread the wrapping paper on top of it and, taking the pencil carefully in hand, began to write slowly, spelling the words aloud as he wrote: "A-l-b-e-r-t L-o-n-g. A-b-r-a-h-a-m L-i-n-c-o-l-n. You see? Both our names begin with the letters, A and L. Guess our paths were meant to cross in this world."

Albert stared at the paper. "Is that supposed to be me?"

"That's you, big as life and twice as handsome."

The boy could hardly believe it. The words

written in the careful script looked far too fine to have anything to do with him.

"Would it always be me, and nothing else, if it was written just that way?"

Abe nodded solemnly. "If you saw those two words in New York or China, they wouldn't say jimmy-crack-corn or pig-in-a-poke. They'd always say 'Albert Long.'"

Albert snickered in spite of himself, then looked suspicious.

"I don't hardly see how you can write my name, just meeting me and all."

Abe explained about the alphabet. If a person knew all twenty-six letters and knew how to put them together in different ways, he could write anything in the world he pleased.

"I wish I could do it," Albert said enviously.

Abe lifted his eyebrows. "Why not? The Lord gave you a head, didn't he? And I reckon, like as not, He put a brain in it. A brain is somewhat like this here candle though—it's no good till you put a light to it. Learning is a light. Take ahold here—"

Albert grasped the pencil tightly while Abe put his hand on top to guide.

"This is *A*, the first letter of the alphabet and the first letter of your name and mine. Go up tall with your *l* and *b* . . . down and around for *e* . . . across with *r* and up again for *t*. Make a little line there—that's called crossing your *t*. Now we're ready for the second name. The big *L*, capital *L*, they call it, is a handsome fellow. He loops this way and that. Next, make a round *o*, and this is *n* and finish off with a pretty *g*, and there you are— Albert Long."

The owner of the name looked at the paper. He had *signed* it!

"Again!" he begged.

They went over it again and again, then Albert wanted to try it alone. Abe gave him a lump of hard brown sugar to suck as he worked. The store was quiet once more.

After a long time Albert stopped writing and straightened up. His back was tired from bending over the paper; his hand was cramped from gripping the pencil. Over and over he had written the ten letters of his name until the writing looked pretty good. It would get better, because he intended to keep practicing at home. He had it now and he would never forget it. All his life he would be able to sign his name. When he was a man, he wouldn't have to make his mark while somebody else signed for him. He felt good.

Albert stood up and stretched. Abe was deep in another newspaper. Quietly the boy crossed the room. Between the dress goods and the chinaware, there was a shelf which held needles, pins, thread, yellow hard soap and half a dozen old books. Curiously he pulled each book out a little way, peeking first at the cover, then inside at the pages. Finally he chose the one which looked most interesting, took it out and began to thumb through it, pausing over the queer sketches of birds and animals, wishing he could make out the words.

"You're mighty curious about books for a boy who says reading isn't worth much." Abe was studying him with a smile.

Albert closed the book quickly. "I just like to look at the pictures," he said stubbornly.

Abe yawned. "Pictures are all right—reading's better."

"Where did you get so many books anyway?"

The clerk unfolded himself and ambled over. "Borrowed mostly, but there aren't anyways near as many as I'd like. They say that up in Indianapolis, our new state capital, there are hundreds of books. Think of it! All waiting to be read. I hear they paid a fellow nine dollars and fifty cents to cart the law books up there from the old capital at Corydon. Wish't they had let me have the job; I would have carted them for nothing."

Remembering what Hoggy Jenks said about Abe reading when he should have been shucking corn, Albert figured it was a good thing he hadn't got the job. Likely he would have pulled off the road somewhere, started reading, and those law books never would have got to Indianapolis.

Abe was passing his hands over the tops of the books, calling out the name of each as if it was a personal friend—*Pilgrim's Progress, Webster's Spelling Book,* the *Bible, Robinson Crusoe, Statutes of Indiana, Life of George Washington, Aesop's Fables,* and *History of the United States.*

Albert reached for the last book and turned to the picture on the first page. It looked familiar.

"What's this place?"

"That's the White House in Washington where our president, Andy Jackson, lives. 'Old Hickory,' they call him. He's the first president really elected by the people and the first to come from plain folks. He was born in a log cabin, just like you and me."

Albert wondered aloud if he and Abe would ever see the White House.

"Oh, we may." Abe declared. "The Lord works in mysterious ways, His wonders to perform."

It was turning out to be a good day after all. Albert hated to see it end, but any minute Pa might reappear, saying it was time to start for home.

"How long before they're back with the wagons?" He looked anxiously toward the door.

Abe assured him it would be quite a spell yet.

"They started early. I expect they'll get clear to Rockport before they spy those wagons, and that's a pretty fair piece on foot. The boats may not even be in yet."

Albert wasn't sorry about being left behind now, even if it meant missing the town of Rockport. More questions kept popping into his head, and he wanted time for Abe to answer them. If only the clerk didn't say he had better be getting back to work.

"What's this one?" He pointed to the book with the drawings of birds and animals.

"That's *Aesop's Fables.* Aesop was a Greek slave who lived long before Christ. He wrote stories with morals to them. Did you ever hear about 'The Fox and the Grapes'?"

"Tell it to me."

Abe leaned back against the shelves and began to read:

A hungry fox once saw some fine, luscious grapes hanging from a vine a few feet above his head. He leaped and snapped and leaped again, but he could never quite reach the grapes. So many times did he try that he tired himself out completely, and it was some time before he could drag himself limping away. As he went along he grumbled savagely to himself: 'What nasty things those grapes are. No gentleman would eat a thing so sour.'

Abe closed the book. "Do you know what the moral of that story is?"

Albert laughed. "Sure, I do. That old fox wanted those grapes in the worst way, but when he saw that he couldn't have them, he just pretended that they were no-account."

Abe's eyes twinkled. "You're somewhat like that old fox, Albert Long."

The boy was puzzled. "How do you figure it?"

"Why, you say sour grapes to schooling, because you think it is out of your reach."

Albert looked away in embarrassment. Abe was a regular wizard. Though he hadn't meant to admit his disappointment to anyone, he found himself telling Abe all about his interest in school, his many attempts to persuade his father, and Pa's stubborn refusal.

As he talked, Abe kept nodding as if he understood.

"Just like my pa," he said when Albert finished. "If it hadn't been for my stepmother, I wouldn't have any schooling to speak of. What I do have doesn't amount to more than a year, all told, and I got that just by littles."

The mention of Abe's stepmother reminded

Albert of his own mother and of his unkept promise to learn to read the Bible. He told Abe about it.

"She never held me to it," he hastened to add, "and I expect she's forgot, but I haven't. It would be a pleasure to her if I could read just a little bit of it. I doubt if I could learn though. I've looked into it, and the words seem awful hard."

"Everything is hard till you learn it," Abe scoffed. "Then it's easy."

Reaching over his head to the top shelf, he took down the big black book with the worn leather cover and began to turn the thin pages slowly as if searching for something in particular.

"Here it is. The Book of John in the New Testament, eleventh chapter, thirty-fifth verse. It's the shortest verse in the Bible, just two words."

They sat down with their heads together, repeating the words, spelling them out, writing them on a piece of brown paper, over and over. Finally Albert could open the Bible, turn to the right page and read aloud: "John 11:35, Jesus wept." He could write it, too.

Abe praised him for being a quick learner, and Albert blushed with pride as he tucked the Bible verse into his pocket beside the paper with his name on it. Miracles, miracles, just like the ones in the Bible. On this common, ordinary day in October, 1829, he had learned to read and write. He had proved that he could do it. Rather, Abe had proved it. He looked admiringly at his new friend and wondered why this smart fellow was wasting his time clerking in Gentry's store.

"How come you don't teach school? You know everything."

Abe's face turned glum. "I don't though. Oh, I can read and write and cipher some, and that's more than most folks around here can do. But if I started in to teach, the well would soon run dry. There's lots more I need to know. Take grammar, for instance. Sometimes I forget and say ain't."

"What's wrong with that?"

Abe looked stern as a schoolmaster. "It ain't, I mean, it *isn't* right."

"It ain't?" Albert asked in surprise.

"It *isn't*," Abe corrected him firmly.

Albert made a mental note to remember that fact. There was a lot in the world to learn, he could see that.

"What would you be, Abe, if you could be anything you wanted?"

The clerk leaned back, hands locked behind his head, eyes dreamy, and thought about it.

"A lawyer, I guess. A lawyer in a plug hat and white collar. Every chance I get, I go down to Rockport and Booneville and listen to them argue in the courts. Then I might get into politics. That's where a fellow has a chance to make a name for himself by writing speeches and giving them all over the state. But I don't have anyways near enough education for that."

The rugged face grew suddenly somber as if a dark cloud had passed over it. Albert had noticed that his expression could change from happy to gloomy in the wink of an eye. Right now he was staring into space, brooding, as if the whole world was set against him. For several minutes neither of them spoke. Albert didn't know how to get through to a person who seemed so far away.

"Well, where could you go to get more education?" he asked finally, not sure he would get an answer.

Abe came to. "Oh, up in Indianapolis, I guess, or Vandalia, the capital of Illinois."

It was hard to pull up stakes and go that far, Albert agreed.

Abe walked to the doorway and stared out at the woods, glowing golden red in the morning sunlight.

"My pa and family are fixing to move to Illinois in the spring." He said it softly as if he were telling it to himself. "He's been after me to go along, but I guess I won't. I guess I'll stay here and work for Gentry or be a farmhand or a blacksmith. I'll just be a piece of floating driftwood and lodge where I land."

Albert thought he had never heard a fellow sound so discouraged. When he answered Abe, though, he said the wrong thing.

"Seems to me a boy ought to go where his pa tells him."

Abe whirled around, scowling. "Not when a boy is almost of age. I'll be twenty-one come February, and I can stop turning over my pay to my father and stop taking his orders, too. He and I never see eye to eye on anything. If I stick with him and go up to Illinois, I'll never get any more learning. Work is all he knows. Well, he taught me to work with my hands, but he forgot to teach me to like it. I'd rather work with my head."

Abe folded up again in the rocking chair. The black cat padded toward him. Albert saw it coming and jumped aside, but Abe reached down and scooped it up into his lap and began to pet it.

"Don't you hate to have that creature around?" Albert exclaimed. "Black cats are the worst kind of bad luck. One has been hanging around our cabin lately. I reckon that's what caused all our trouble."

Abe stroked the cat defiantly. "That's just a superstition," he growled. "Folks mostly make their own luck in this world. If you don't get to school,

Albert Long, don't blame it on this poor cat. If you are determined to become a student, you will. Once a person makes up his mind, he is more than half-way there."

"How come you don't just make up your mind to be a lawyer?" he asked pertly.

Abe scowled again. "I told you. I want to be as free from my pa as this here cat."

Now Albert knew how to get to school. He would ask Abe to speak to Pa about it. If his father still didn't give in, Albert planned to walk to Pigeon Creek and study with Abe and get his education "by littles." Thank the Lord, Abe was going to stay in Indiana. Still, Albert couldn't help wanting to argue back.

"I guess you'll never be a lawyer then," he prodded, " 'cause our preacher says, 'God helps those that help themselves.' "

The gray eyes under the shaggy eyebrows glared at him, then closed. The clerk slumped farther down in the chair, his lower lip stuck out. He was half-thinking, half-pouting. He appeared to be a world away. Scanning the books, Albert took down the one Abe had called *Life of George Washington*. It was warped, wrinkled and bent, with its pages spotted and stained.

"Looks like it got caught in a cyclone." He waited anxiously.

There was no answer from the figure in the

rocking chair. Not a sound. The dark, craggy face with its dropped eyelids remained still, as if in a doze.

He's mad at me for good, thought Albert. I wish I'd kept my mouth shut.

"I guess it isn't much of a book anyway." He set it back on the shelf.

One gray eye opened, then the other. The clerk sat up, wide-awake.

"It's one of my favorites, but it caused me a lot of trouble when it got rained on accidentally."

"What happened?"

"I had borrowed it from our neighbor, Josiah Crawford. When he saw it, he set up a terrible howl. Made me pull fodder three days to pay for it. I still admire George Washington, but I don't care much for old Blue Nose Crawford."

They were no longer alone. A shadow fell across the doorway, and a throat was cleared noisily.

Abe leaped up. "Why, Mr. Crawford! I was just thinking about you."

The man with the huge, purplish nose looked suspiciously from the clerk to the boy.

"Your pa wants you, Abe," he said sharply. "Somebody in your vicinity needs a chicken house moved."

"I'm supposed to be minding this store," Abe stalled.

Old Blue Nose narrowed his eyes, "You know when your pa says now, he means now." It sounded like a threat.

Abe sighed. "Yep. I reckon I better hightail it over there."

The man eased himself into the rocking chair. "I'll keep a weather eye on the store."

"Help yourself to my paper," Abe said generously.

Blue Nose Crawford gave him a hard look. "Abe Lincoln," he spoke as if dealing with an idiot, "some folks got better things to do with their time than fooling around, reading." He closed his eyes for a nap.

Slapping his straw hat on his head, Abe called out, "Come on, Albert, let's make tracks."

Halfway to the door, he remembered the turkey and something else. From under the counter he drew out a small book and tucked it into his back pocket. Albert picked up a piece of charcoal and put it in his pocket. If Abe was going to read, he would practice his writing. The two of them hurried out of the store without looking back. They knew that Blue Nose had been listening at the doorway and hadn't liked what he heard. Not everybody in Pigeon Creek admired Abe Lincoln.

5

The tall man approached the cabin. "Hello, the House!"

He pulled his hat down over his forehead and spoke in a low, unnatural voice.

" 'Morning, ma'am. Would you like to take a gander at my pretty chinee dishes, shiny pans, needles, pins, thread? There must be something you need today."

Inside the cabin the short, plump woman paused to wipe her hands on her apron.

"We need everything, peddler, but cash is mighty scarce. I wouldn't mind looking at your

70

wares though." She turned toward the door.

"Abe Lincoln! You scamp! Shame on you for fooling your poor old mammy." She laughed at him and at herself for being taken in. "Thought you was working at the store."

"I was, but Pa had to send for me to do some chore nobody else wanted to do."

His mother held out both hands to him. "Come in first and set a minute," she said sympathetically. "Something to eat will give you strength and the green tomato pies I baked for supper are still hot. I reckon I can spare half a pie for a hungry boy."

Bustling about, she pulled a chair up to the table, brushed off crumbs, and made everything tidy. Then she caught sight of the boy lagging behind Abe.

"Why, you brought a visitor."

Abe pulled him forward. "This here is Albert Long from Pokeberry Creek. His pa went down to wait for the wagons, and Albert is giving me the favor of his company. This bird is a present to you from him."

Mrs. Lincoln threw up her hands in delight. "Bless your sweet heart. I've just been craving me some turkey."

"I might let Albert move that chicken house while I finish my study of elocution and public speaking." Abe touched the little book in his back pocket.

Mrs. Lincoln protested that he would do no such thing. Albert was company, and he was going to be treated so.

"Set right down, Albert, and eat some pie. Such a likely looking boy . . ." her bright blue eyes rested on him fondly, "I always did admire a boy with freckles."

Her gaze moved to Abe, and her smile faded.

"Seems but a minute since you was his age. Now look at you. You're going through another one of your thin spells. Have another piece of pie. It will put some meat on your bones."

Abe shook his head. "Better get going on that chicken house." He stood and stretched.

"I declare, son, you've growed another inch since yesterday. Your head's fairly brushing the ceiling. Mind you keep that head clean," she teased. "I can scrub your footprints off my floor, but my ceiling is freshly whitewashed."

Affectionately she reached up and rumpled his hair.

Albert was glad to see her act this way. Sometimes he thought that his own mother treated him like a baby, yet here was big Abe's mother acting just the same. Mothers were all alike.

Now she was hurrying about, gathering up

victuals and dishes and putting them into a basket.

"I'm sorry to have to leave you boys, but Mrs. Brooner had her baby last night, and I promised I would take her some soup and sassafras and honey and an extra blanket, in case it turns cold in the night."

Abe waved her on. "We'll be getting along. Pa will be looking in soon to make sure I'm working and not loafing or reading. They are the same thing to him, of course."

Mrs. Lincoln stopped and gave her son a long look. "Don't be hard on your pa, Abe. He means well."

After his mother had left the cabin, he walked back and forth, gazing at the clean, white ceiling. There was a queer glint in his eye.

"Hey, Albert, want to see something funny?"

Albert looked up. He didn't see anything special.

"Remember what Ma said about my head touching the ceiling? And I said it was a good thing my feet aren't where my head is?"

Albert laughed.

"Come outside and take off your moccasins."

Albert obeyed, though he didn't understand.

"Walk around in this mud puddle."

Albert stared.

"Go ahead—walk."

He began to tramp around in the puddle. The mud felt cool and good to his feet which were getting blacker and blacker.

"That's fine."

Before Albert could say *Jack Robinson,* he was picked up like a sack of potatoes and turned upside-down. Now he was goggling at the moving ground as his feet waved wildly in the air. The next thing he knew his bare, dirty feet were planted firmly on Mrs. Lincoln's clean, white ceiling.

"Walk!"

"Abe, put me down! You're crazy! She'll kill me! My pa will kill me!"

"Walk!"

Albert couldn't help himself. With Abe's urging, he walked all over that ceiling. When at last he was set down, right-side-up, the ceiling was a sight to see. Small black footprints were tracked everywhere as though a giant fly with a boy's feet had been exploring overhead.

Abe looked at the prints and chuckled. He bent over and held his sides and laughed so long and loud that Albert, scared as he was of what Mrs. Lincoln would say, couldn't help laughing, too. Finally Abe choked, "Come on, Albert. Let's move that henhouse."

The shortcut through the woods passed by a grove of sassafras trees. A little breeze stirred the trees and wafted their sweet, spicy smell. Albert reached out and caught a leaf. He bruised it between his fingers and held it to his nose, savoring the familiar scent. Orange-colored sassafras tea was good for almost any ailment. It was fine if you were chilled or had a fever and it thinned the blood in the spring. His mother always kept some on hand. Now Abe's mother was carrying some to her neighbor who had a new baby.

Mrs. Lincoln was a nice woman like his own mother. Albert felt a twinge of guilt when he thought of her ruined ceiling. Wasn't that a pretty way to repay her for her kindness and her pie.

"Your ma is nice, Abe."

"She sure is."

The cheerful voice didn't sound a bit sorry. Either he had forgotten the ceiling or didn't give a hoot.

"She's a good soul. We get along fine, her and me. She's about the only one in the family I do get along with," he added grimly. "It's queer it should be that way, because she's only my stepmother and Pa is my real father."

Abe looked hard at his companion, as if an outsider might solve the problem. Albert didn't know what to say, but he did notice that whenever Abe mentioned his father, a dark cloud passed over his face.

Without warning, Abe cut off from the path and climbed a little hill to a clearing. He stopped and stared down at a mound of earth covered with brown grass and a few autumn leaves.

"Who is buried here?" Albert's voice was hushed in respect for the dead.

"My real mother. She died of the milksick when I was nine. She was good and kind like my stepmother. If I ever amount to anything, I'll owe it all to those two women."

Abe remembered the day his mother died. There was a log left over from building the cabin. His father whipped it into planks for a coffin, and nine-year-old Abe whittled the pinewood pegs with his jackknife.

"We carried her up to this little hill where there is shade and sun, too. I helped pick the spot. Once I saw a doe and her fawn step lightly over the grave. Gentle creatures with soft, dark eyes like hers. After that, it seemed I could never pull a trigger on a deer."

"Let's go, Abe."

The tall young man didn't hear. He stepped forward and straightened the piece of red sandstone that marked the grave.

"Her name was Nancy. I guess this place is one thing that holds me in Indiana. I come here sometimes and lean against that tree and read, and nobody ever bothers me."

He stood straight. "Yes, Albert, let's go."

Off down the path he went, his head held high. He was his old cheerful self, the somber moments behind him.

Trotting along the narrow footpath, with the bright, autumn foliage pressing close on either side, Albert kept his eyes moving to the right, to the left, as he listened for a rustle that was more than blowing leaves.

"What would you do if an Indian jumped you right now, Abe?"

"Jump him back, I reckon. Wrestle him to the ground. Try to get his hatchet before he buried it in my head."

"Would you scalp him with it?"

"Scalp him? Heck, no, Albert. It's all I can do to skin a possum."

"Well, would you kill him or take him prisoner?"

Abe considered it. "I would do whatever seemed best. I sure hate fighting and killing, but sometimes the most peaceful fellow is forced to fight to protect himself and his loved ones. I wouldn't just stand still and let an Indian do to me what one did to my Grandpa Abraham back in Kentucky."

Albert gulped. "What did he do?"

Abe told the old story. An Indian had sneaked up and killed his grandfather right in plain sight of his cabin. Abe's father, Tom Lincoln, had seen it happen. He was just a little boy. The Indian picked up Tom, fixing to run away with him, but Tom's older brother, Mordecai, who was about Albert's age at the time, came running with his gun and shot the savage dead. From that time on, it was said, Uncle Mordecai Lincoln would shoot any Indian on sight and ask questions afterwards.

"Now that was a mistake," Abe mused. "He might have shot a good Indian."

Albert remembered that he had left his gun back at Gentry's store. A lot of good it would do him there. Without it, he felt as helpless as a beetle on its back. Abe could protect the two of them from almost any danger, but what if Abe were attacked?

Thank goodness, they were now coming out of the woods into a patch of sunlight. Ahead there were six log cabins in the clearing. They had been built close to each other, as if the families who lived in them had huddled together for company and protection. Albert knew his father wouldn't stand living that close to another man's dwelling. Pa liked air and space and land around him, but then Pa wasn't afraid of Indians or wild animals or anything else.

"Yonder's the place where we're to move the henhouse," Abe pointed.

"Abe Lincoln!"

He stopped. "Who calls? Oh, howdy, Mrs. Miller."

The young woman stood in the doorway of the first cabin, balancing a baby on her hip.

"How's little Silas today? I see he survived my tender care." Abe chuckled as he stroked the fat baby under the chin.

"His colic is lots better, Abe. And I want to thank you for tending him and the other children while I was away. I hope they wasn't much trouble to you."

"No trouble," Abe assured her. "All I had to do was rock the cradle with my foot. I just read and rocked, read and rocked. You ought to try it some time."

Mrs. Miller laughed. "Go on, Abe! You know I can't read a word. But sometimes I do sew and rock. We're so thankful for all your help to us since the accident. I crave to do something to pay you back for your kindness."

She looked critically at his old worn trousers, which were shrunk halfway to his knees.

"You could use some new jeans, I notice."

Abe looked down at his patched trousers, which were mighty scrubby looking.

"I got some nice cloth here that I wove myself and dyed with walnut bark," Mrs. Miller went on.

"I'd be glad to make you a new pair of pants, if you're willing."

His face lighted up. "Yes, ma'am, I'd be happy for them."

She told him to come back next week and the garment would be ready.

"I'll just make the longest britches for the longest legs in Indiana, and they'll be all right."

"Mrs. Miller shouldn't bother with me," Abe told Albert as they walked on. "A widow with six little ones—poor soul. Her husband was killed in an accident in the woods when a tree fell on him."

When they reached the third log cabin in the clearing, Abe circled around to the fenced-in back lot. At his sudden appearance, a grimy sow hustled her pink pigs away. A flock of banty chickens flapped and squawked their way across the yard, some running into the cabin as if they lived there.

"Hello, the House! Anybody home? It's Abe Lincoln, come to steal your chickens."

A shadow filled the doorway. "I ain't scared of that. You wouldn't steal a biscuit if you was starving."

The big man with the red face and the whisky breath came out into the yard, followed by the other men, all shouting greetings.

As if he had no time to lose, Abe asked, "Where do you want your henhouse moved to?"

80

"There's no need to rush the job," the man insisted. "Come inside first and have a drink of applejack. It will strengthen you."

Abe shook his head. "On the contrary, it would make me feel all weak and undone."

The red-faced man laughed and said that Abe was just like his father.

"Never could get Tom to take a drink with me neither."

It was like his father, too, Albert thought. Mr. Long always said there was something wrong with a man who had to get through his days by swigging whisky.

Abe was rolling up his sleeves. "Where did you say you wanted her moved?"

The owner pointed toward the far corner of the lot. He was planning to move the fence out, he explained, and make the whole yard bigger. That way, the chickens would keep in their place and his wife wouldn't complain about them flapping in and out of the cabin.

"The way I see it, Abe, we'll slip these two poles under the henhouse, and then we'll put a fellow at each corner to lift. With your help, four of us ought to manage it, though it's awful heavy. Two hundred pounds, I guess."

Stepping up to the henhouse, Abe looked it over carefully. He stretched out his long arms and wrapped them around the house, measuring its size. The other men took deep breaths and flexed their muscles, getting ready to help. Before any one of them could speak, Abe lifted the henhouse off the ground and began to carry it across the yard. Slowly, carefully he moved, until he reached the far corner of the lot where he set it down.

"This where you want it?"

The man's mouth dropped open. He turned to his friends.

"Did you see what I saw?"

They nodded, speechless.

"I swan, Abe, there ain't another fellow in these parts could have moved that by himself."

They clustered around him, feeling his muscles, praising his strength. The power of speech came back to them, all at once.

"Say, I got a little job over at my place . . ."

"Me, too, we're having a house-raising."

One farmer stepped forward, ahead of the rest. "How about killing a hog for me next week? I'll pay you."

Abe considered this offer. "All right," he gave in, "if you risk the hog, I'll risk myself."

The henhouse owner followed him out to the gate, thanking him all the way for his help. He wanted Abe to understand that he would have moved that henhouse all by himself.

"But I ain't as strong as I used to be."

Abe smiled. "Lay off that applejack and you'll be as good a man as you ever were. That's all right," he added kindly as he saw the man's embarrassment, "I was glad to help out."

When they were out of sight of the cabin, Albert couldn't hold back his praise. What Abe had done was great. He was convinced that his friend could be anything he wanted to be. He thought Abe would be pleased with the compliment, but the tall angular fellow only grunted.

"Oh, sure I can. Abe Lincoln—flatboatman, grocery clerk, baby-rocker, rail-splitter, henhouse-mover, hog-killer—I've never done anything important, to make anyone know I ever lived."

They swerved off the path and cut into the woods, stepping as lightly as Indians behind the cabins. Albert hoped they weren't going to visit the grave again. In the woodlot behind the Miller cabin Abe stopped. He looked at the heap of logs laying there, tumbled every which way. He kept looking until he spied an axe near the woodpile. Picking up the tool, he held it at arm's length, testing its weight.

"Stand back now."

Lifting the axe high in the air, Abe brought it down squarely in the middle of a log which split neatly in half as if it had been ordered to do so. He kicked the pieces to one side and tackled the next log, then the next.

"How come you're cutting Mrs. Miller's wood for her? She didn't ask you to."

Abe wiped the sweat out of his eyes.

"She should have asked me though. I'm not going to take a fine new pair of pants just for rocking her baby. With no man in the house, these logs would stand uncut all winter. And what would she do for firewood to keep those children warm?"

As he worked, Albert sat on a nearby stump, watching, listening, his ears tuned to the forest, as usual, for a rustle or a footstep. His ears tingled from listening so hard. The hair on the back of his neck prickled as he thought of the Pigeon Roost massacre. He must try to forget that and the story of Abe's grandpa, too. No Indians around here anymore, he said to himself over and over.

The long brown arms with the knotted muscles swung the axe up and down, splitting each log evenly, never missing. Abe could be tough if he wanted. He could be a bully like the rivermen, or like Cousin Hiram. But he was tougher than those fellows because he was not only strong enough to outfight them all, he was smart enough to outtalk them. He knew that he was, too. Albert guessed that was the reason Abe didn't have to get tough often. It was only the people who weren't sure of themselves who had to push other folks around.

If I were as smart and strong as Abe, Albert thought enviously, I wouldn't be afraid of anything!

But he wasn't. He still wished for his gun in the woods. He wasn't afraid of everything. Just savages and bears. What he was most afraid of though, was being a coward. In time of real danger, he wanted to believe that he would have the nerve to stand his ground and fight his way out like Abe or Pa would. In a pinch, he reckoned he might just turn tail and run like a jackrabbit, but he wasn't sure.

Albert tensed as he heard a noise. The bushes behind Abe rustled. Out of the brush came a whoop and a cry. A body leaped forward, hurling itself at the woodsman. The axe flew into the air, and Abe hollered as he was pulled to the ground.

Albert grabbed for his rifle. It wasn't there. Dashing forward, he threw himself on top of Abe and the body. The flashing axe descended upon a bare, brown leg, and blood spurted, staining the oak leaves scarlet. Albert grasped the squirming attacker by the neck.

"I've got him, Abe!" he cried triumphantly. "Run for help!"

6

Albert had such a good hold on the attacker, it was hard to understand why Abe kept tugging and jerking and yelling, "Let go, Albert! Let go!"

Abe gave a final pull, and the startled boy rolled over in the leaves and sat up, staring at the stranger who stared back at him. It was a girl! A girl with short black hair and skin sun-browned as an Indian. As she sat there, she began to sob, as if she was scared to death, and clutch her leg which was bleeding like a stuck pig all over her linsey-woolsey dress.

"What kind of tomfoolery are you up to?"

Abe gasped. "Don't you know you liked to got killed?"

The girl tried to answer, but she was making so much noise with her blubbering that they couldn't understand her. Finally she managed to choke out a few words.

"I just wanted to scare you."

Abe dropped down beside her, still shaking.

"You sure succeeded." He was both frightened and angry. "Albert here has been filling my head so full of Injun talk, I thought for sure you were a savage. You're lucky that axe only grazed your leg. If I'da had a firm grip on it, I'da swung it at you, and then where would you be?"

He looked sternly at the girl who was drying her tears on the hem of her skirt. His expression grew soft.

"Here, let me look at that leg." He examined it carefully. "Oh, it's not as bad as I feared. It's a long cut but not very deep." He pulled a rag from his pocket. "This here is pretty clean. It'll do till you get home."

Gently, he bound the girl's leg, taking care not to hurt her. When he was through, he put his arm about her shoulder, but his voice was still stern.

"Next time you get an idea, stop first and think."

She hung her head. "I'll try."

Abe looked up. "Are you still with us, Albert? Or did you faint dead away?"

"I'm here."

Abe studied him with approval. "I guess you wouldn't faint. You were pretty brave. Well, meet my stepsister, Tilda Johnson. She isn't always this much trouble. Most of the time, she's a pretty good gal."

"Howdy," Albert muttered. He stared right over her head, up into the treetops. Maybe she would catch on to his dislike for her. The nitwit. His heart was still pounding. How could Abe be nice to a nincompoop who had caused so much trouble? What he hated most about her was that, after all the trouble, she wasn't an Indian.

Abe seemed to read his mind. "Everybody makes mistakes, Albert." He helped his sister to her feet and asked if she could get home by herself.

"I can make it, but Abe," she clutched at his arm and her eyes looked scared again, "what will I tell Pa? He's going to be awful mad. Help me make up a story to tell him."

Her stepbrother shook his head. "Tell him the truth. It stands up better and gets you out of trouble sooner than anything else."

Tilda nodded but Albert wondered if she would

have the nerve to follow the good advice, or if she would make up a fib that would get them both in bad with Mr. Lincoln.

After she hobbled off, Abe went back to work. He chopped and Albert stacked until they had a big pile of wood of all sizes and kinds. There were chips to kindle a low fire, brush to make a blaze, and huge backlogs to keep a fireplace roaring night and day.

"This will make a start for her." Abe laid down the axe. "I can finish the rest some other time."

Widow Miller would be surprised at this kind deed. "Aren't you going to tell her who did it?" Albert wondered.

"I expect she'll know."

A little piece down the road they passed a nice, hewed-log building with oilpaper windows. Abe seemed proud to point it out as the Pigeon Creek Baptist Church, which his father had helped build.

"We'd be pleased to have you and your folks visit it sometime," he offered, "even if you aren't Baptists. I wish you could have heard the preacher take out after slavery last Sunday. Baptists are great antislavery people, you know."

Albert guessed maybe his family was Baptist

then, because his father sure was opposed to slave-holding. That was the reason the Longs had moved up to free Indiana. Here, every man was his own boss. Nobody was called a "scrub" just because he didn't own other folks to plow and plant for him. Down South, he had heard his father say, white men who didn't own slaves were about as bad off as the slaves themselves.

Albert hoped he could bring his parents to the Pigeon Creek Church some Sunday. It had been a long time since any circuit riding preachers had come around Pokeberry Creek, and they were usually Methodists.

"Which church do you think is best, Abe?"

The young man answered quickly, "The one that says: Thou shalt love the Lord with all thy heart and thy neighbor as thyself. That's the church for me."

A preacher couldn't have said it better.

Swinging along the path behind Abe's long stride, Albert thought about this unusual day. A day to remember through the long, cold, monotonous winter. It seemed that his life had taken a different turn since early morning when he and his father had started their journey. First, there was the reading of Peabody's crooked paper, and the farewell to the boots and other good things that he and Pa had thought were in their grasp.

90

But getting acquainted with Abe was good. He had made up his mind to be as near like Abe as possible, even to try to grow as tall and strong. If he went to the orchard every day and hung by his hands from a limb, maybe he could stretch his height. Secretly, he made a fist and felt his upper arm. Chopping wood, digging out stumps, plowing, spading, lifting, would develop his muscle. Never again would he complain when his mother asked him to fill the woodbox or tote water from the creek.

While he was dreaming of following in Abe's footsteps, he wondered guiltily if it was right for a boy to want to be more like another man than his own father. Albert was curious to know if Abe took after his father.

Abe turned his head. "Let's stop by my place and see if my mother wants something from the store."

7

Nobody was home at the Lincoln cabin, but the footprints were still there. They made such a crazy sight, running higgledy-piggledy over the ceiling, Albert couldn't keep from grinning. His grin faded when he thought of what Abe's mother and father would say. Shutting his eyes, he rubbed the buckeye in his pocket with one hand and the rabbit's foot with the other, wishing hard that the tracks would disappear.

Abe was looking around outside, peering this way and that, until he spied a big bucket with a stick in it. He stirred the contents vigorously, then carried the pail into the cabin and set it by the fireplace. From the doorway, Albert watched uneasily, hoping it wouldn't be another trick.

Someone was coming. Hastily, he backed out of the door, feeling the need to put more space between himself and that ceiling. Voices from the woods grew closer and louder. A man's voice and a woman's and the high tones of a young girl were in some kind of argument.

"Quit standing up for him. I'm sick and tired of his foolishness."

Coming out of the woods into the cabin lot, they stopped in surprise when they saw Albert.

"You fellows back from your errand so soon?" Mrs. Lincoln beamed.

"Howdy, ma'am." Albert glanced at Tilda, who stood beside her mother, favoring one leg like a lame chicken. He guessed he would have to speak to her, too.

"Howdy," he muttered.

She didn't reply but only stared at him sheepishly and sucked her fingers.

Abe's mother turned to the man. "Tom, this here is Albert Long, Abe's friend from Pokeberry Creek."

The boy looked up at Mr. Lincoln. This was

Abe's pa, all right. He was shorter than his son but strong built, and he had the same little squint in one eye that Abe had.

Mr. Lincoln stretched out a rough hand and rumpled Albert's hair. "Hey there, boy." He smiled down. "Pleased to meet you."

Albert relaxed. He could tell right off whether a person really liked boys or was only pretending. But now Mr. Lincoln was looking around suspiciously.

"Where is that son of mine?"

Albert jerked his thumb toward the cabin.

"Here I am, Pa," Abe answered from the doorway.

His father glared at him. "Yes, there you are. Are you hiding in there? I don't wonder. You got call to be ashamed."

To Albert's surprise, Tilda hobbled forward and clutched the man's arm.

"Please, Pa, don't abuse Abe. I told you how the accident happened. It was my fault, and that's the truth."

He shook her off. "Yes, she's been taking the blame, but I ain't sure I believe her story. She might be trying to cover up for you, the way women-folks do. I bet two cents this cut on her leg comes from some durn-fool prank of yours."

Abe looked at his father glumly and didn't

offer a word in his own defense. Albert's face grew hot. He wanted to holler out that Abe was in the right, that Tilda's story was true. He felt a new respect for her since her confession. Looking at Mr. Lincoln's stern face, he knew it wouldn't do any good. Abe's father was the kind of man who believed what he believed. Nothing would change him.

"Come on, folks, let's go inside," Mrs. Lincoln said nervously.

Albert followed the family into the cabin, lagging as far behind as possible. At first, nobody noticed anything unusual. Tilda limped over to a chair and sat down, rubbing her leg and making painful faces. She was going to get all the sympathy she could out of her injury. Mr. Lincoln stood at the door, looking out, cold and silent. Mrs. Lincoln set her empty basket on the table, removed her sunbonnet and smoothed her hair. She was tying on her calico apron when she happened to glance upward.

"Oh. Did you ever! If that don't beat all!"

Every head turned and followed her eye upward. For a long minute not a word was said. Albert backed into a corner, hoping they would forget his presence.

Like a bear, a growl started low in Mr. Lincoln's throat and grew louder until it was a roar.

"What in tarnation?"

Mrs. Lincoln threw her apron over her head and her shoulders began to shake. Tilda giggled. Abe chuckled. Albert looked from one to the other, shocked that they didn't care that their mother was crying. Presently, she pulled the apron down and looked again at the ceiling. She was not crying but laughing so hard that tears stood in her eyes.

"Abe—Abe—" she gasped, "what in the world is going to become of you?" She threw her arms around him and hugged him.

"What's going to become of me?" her stepson repeated, wiping his own eyes. "Why I'm going to be President of the United States!"

At this, both of them started laughing again, fit to kill, until Albert forgot all his worry and laughed with them. The high jinks stopped when they felt a hard stare of disapproval. His scowl was a dash of cold water.

"Well, you've had your fun," Mr. Lincoln said, "though, for the life of me, I can't see anything funny in such goings-on." His accusing gaze rested on Abe. "I suppose you're going to tell me that Tilda is responsible for this, too."

"No, Pa, I'm responsible. It was just a little joke between Ma and me."

Mr. Lincoln turned to his wife. "Why don't somebody explain it to me so I can snicker, too?"

He waited, but it seemed that nobody wanted to take the trouble to tickle his funny bone, if he had such a thing.

"Is this what you was wasting time with, when you was supposed to be moving that henhouse?" he asked Abe sourly.

"I've already moved the henhouse, Pa."

The older man seemed disappointed that the deed had been done and he couldn't complain about it. He went to the door and peered out, but couldn't seem to find what he was looking for. He drew his head back and looked all around the cabin.

"There it is. What is it doing in here?"

He picked up the bucket that Abe had set by the fireplace and, from a cranny in the wall, he pulled a wide brush.

"All right, brother," he said grimly, "get busy and cover up your mistakes with this whitewash."

Without a word, Abe took the bucket in one hand and the brush in the other and easily began to paint wide, white swaths across the dirty ceiling.

"Be careful when you come to that beam," his father warned sharply. "Don't paint over my accounts."

Glancing up at the wooden beam with the markings on it, Albert saw that Mr. Lincoln kept his accounts the same way Pa did. When Pa owed somebody money or they owed him, or when he bought or sold something, he would draw a mark on the ceiling beams with a piece of charcoal. When a debt was paid, he would wipe out the mark with a wet rag. It was the closest he could come to arithmetic.

"Keep moving there," Mr. Lincoln ordered. "Don't miss a spot." With every slap of the brush, Abe's face looked redder and madder. Albert didn't blame him a bit. Abe had intended all along to fix the ceiling, but Mr. Lincoln was determined to act as if the paint job was his idea. He was bound he would be the boss. Even now, as he watched the work progress, he didn't seem satisfied. The longer he watched, the more discontented he seemed to be. Stooping at the hearth, he picked up a long stick, and advancing toward his son, he shook it threateningly.

"If it wasn't for the present company, Abe, I'd give you what you deserve."

Abe stopped painting, he set down the bucket, and laid the brush carefully across the top of it. He bent his head so that he could look his father in the eye.

"No, you wouldn't, Pa," he said slowly. "Not in company or in private. Never again."

Mrs. Lincoln threw herself between them. "Oh, Tom! Oh, Abe! Don't fuss so! You're both riled up. Remember that the Bible says, He that ruleth his spirit is greater than he that taketh a city."

Over her head the two men glared at each other. The father was the first to give up. Backing off, he took the stick between his hands and broke it over his knees and hurled the pieces into the fireplace.

"I know what the Bible says," he repeated furiously. "It says, How sharper than a serpent's tooth it is to have a thankless child."

Abe stared at him. "What did you say?"

"You heard me the first time. I said you were ungrateful." Mr. Lincoln was so worked up, he could hardly speak.

"Say it again, Pa, just the way you did before."

"All right, I'll say it again!' he shouted. "How sharper than a serpent's tooth it is to have a thankless child. I heard a preacher say it once, and I remembered it because it sure applies to you."

Abe looked as happy as if he had received the best compliment in the world.

"But it isn't from the Bible," he exclaimed. "It's from the play, *King Lear*, by William Shakespeare. Why, Pa, you're quoting poetry by Shakespeare."

Mr. Lincoln stared at his son and shook his

head. "I don't know what you're talking about, Abe," he said. "I never know what you're talking about anymore."

Albert had been listening carefully, thinking Abe got the best of it in the argument. Mr. Lincoln's shoulders sagged as he turned and walked out the door.

But there was no elation in the young man's face. Abe looked after his father as if he longed to call him back. His expression was one of pure misery. He couldn't have looked unhappier if Mr. Lincoln had beaten him with that stick.

Mrs. Lincoln was bustling about the cabin, making work to keep herself busy. As she puttered about, her lips moved silently as if she were talking over some problem with herself. Seeing her distress, Abe did not resume his painting. Instead, he went over to her, took both her hands in his, and said desperately, "Ma, I can't go to Illinois with you next spring. I'm awful sorry, but I can't go any farther with him. I got to get away."

She patted him. "Whatever you think is best. But why can't you and your pappy get along?"

"I don't know why. I try but I can't get through to him. Now you and me—we get along fine—"

"Yes, what little mind I have seems to run in the same channels as yours. Your pa is a good man though," she added loyally. "There are worse men you could take after. Tom doesn't smoke or drink or swear; he works and pays his debts. Why, you're ever so much like him in some ways, Abe. It's from him that you get your handiness with tools and your knack for telling funny stories."

Abe agreed that he was like his father in some ways. "But not in all ways, and that's what Pa can't bear. He won't even try to understand the ways that I'm not like him."

The two of them got along fine when Abe was little, Mrs. Lincoln remembered. It was just since Abe started growing up that they couldn't talk to each other without scrapping.

"Your father loves you—he's proud of you."

"He has a mighty funny way of showing it."

"I guess he wants to keep you on the straight and narrow path. He's seen so many young fellows your age go wrong. He wants you to be hard-working and God-fearing."

Abe shook his head stubbornly. "No, Ma, he wants me to be father-fearing. He wants to own me till the end of my days. He can't accept the fact that I've grown up. Why, I can't be exactly like him or anybody else. I've got to be myself." He searched her face anxiously. "Can you get along without me up in Illinois?"

"We can," she sighed at last. " 'Course your cousin, Dennis Hanks, ain't much hand to work and your stepbrother, John, ain't got your muscle or brains neither. Your pa will get our cabin built before winter if he ain't too busy hunting and building for other folks. But, yes, we can get along without you. Don't you worry none about us."

Abe was worrying though. Forlornly, his glance swept the tight little cabin as if he wished that he could pick it up like the chicken house, and set it down in the new state of Illinois. He noticed the boy in the corner.

"Albert! I plumb forgot about you. Wouldn't you rather be outside than in here, listening to dull, grown-up talk?"

Albert felt embarrassed to be caught listening.

"I'll help you paint," he offered eagerly. "If you got another brush—"

Abe told him instead to go outside and fill a bag with hickory nuts, butternuts and walnuts, and pick up some ripe paw-paws and persimmons to take home to his mother. The boy scurried out the door, glad to escape the Lincolns' family problems.

The fine day had turned gloomy, though the autumn sun was still shining warmly through the bright woods. The trouble with grown-ups was that they had a way of spoiling everything by talking about troubles that hadn't happened yet. He shuffled about in the dry leaves, searching for nuts that the squirrels had overlooked, taking care not to step on the Indian pipes which rose, pale and ghostly, from the rotting wood beneath the ground. The waxy blossoms, which sprung up so mysteriously overnight, weren't good for anything that he knew of, but he always imagined that it might be bad luck to crush them. Perhaps they marked the grave of an Indian brave, fallen in battle.

"Boy, you're a long way from home."

Mr. Lincoln smiled down at him as if nothing unpleasant had taken place inside the cabin.

"Here, let me show you where to find yourself a nice heap of walnuts."

As they worked side by side, filling the bag, Abe's father kept up an easy patter of conversation. He pointed out the place where Abe had drawn a bead on his first turkey, and told of the time that his son had cornered a raccoon in the hickory tree and had captured him and tamed him.

"He's awful good with animals. They seem to trust him right off. He can't bear to see anything hurt, human or otherwise."

Mr. Lincoln recalled the time that some boys were torturing land turtles and they called Abe to get in on their sport.

"He soon put a stop to that cruel fun!" his father exclaimed. "He just gave those boys what-for.

"Yes, he's so softhearted, it makes him a poor

hunter. Now, I call myself a kind man, but I'm practical, too. A person has to eat, so he has to shoot and fish and trap, and even learn to enjoy them, if he can. Leastways, that's the way I see it. Don't your pa feel the same?"

Mr. Lincoln was looking hard at Albert, as if the boy could tell him whether he was right and Abe was wrong.

Albert hated to take sides against his friend, but he had to tell the truth, especially about hunting.

"My pa feels the same as you, Mr. Lincoln. I do, too. Hunting is one of my favorites."

The man's eyes twinkled, and for a minute he looked like Abe when he was tickled and about to break into a grin.

"I'll bet you're a fine shot, too."

Albert tried to look modest.

"Pretty fair."

It was hard to keep from saying more. If he had Old Surefire, his Pennsylvania rifle, with him, he would show Mr. Lincoln some shooting for his whiskers. He would bark that fox squirrel right out of that hickory tree and send him spinning.

"I imagine you're better than pretty fair," Abe's father guessed shrewdly. "I can usually size up a boy."

The two hunters grinned at each other, the

way people do when they have a common interest. Then the man reached out his hand and laid it on the boy's head and gave a long sigh.

"What's the matter, Mr. Lincoln?"

"Oh, nothing in particular. I was just wishing for a minute that I could turn back the years."

He looked sad. But, like Abe, his gloomy expression didn't stay long. What a great storyteller he was. Albert hoped he could remember all the jokes to tell Pa. They were having such a fine time talking and laughing, they didn't hear the footsteps behind them until a long shadow fell across the leaves.

Abe was a comical sight, his hair, face and clothes spattered with white paint.

"I'm through," he announced brusquely, rolling his sleeves down over his spotted arms.

His father didn't answer. Rising from the stump, he clasped his hands behind his back and stared off into the distance. The three of them stood side by side, gazing silently at the fields and woods beyond.

After a time, Mr. Lincoln cleared his throat. "Uncommon fine weather for near November."

Abe grunted.

"Good weather for finishing outside chores. We must get that roof patched and dig the rest of the potatoes."

"Mighty small potatoes," Abe muttered. "Hardly worth digging."

"Well, I told you we should have planted them in the dark of the moon. Maybe, next year, you'll listen to me."

Abe clasped his hands behind his back like his father.

"Cobwebs on the grass this morning," he changed the subject, "means frost before long."

The older man nodded. "I fear it's going to be a hard winter. Squirrels are laying in more nuts than usual. The caterpillar's coat is awful heavy. Cornhusks are thick . . . so's the apple and onion skins. 'When onion skins are tough, winter will be rough,' " he quoted the old saying.

"I'm partial to warm weather myself," Abe said.

"Yes, I feel somewhat that way," his father agreed, "still, green winters make green graves. I'm always glad to see the first hard frost. It kills off some of the fever."

"Freezing weather is a good thing in that respect," Abe nodded.

Little by little, their conversation became easier and less strained. Albert felt relieved. Abe and his father were on safe ground now. They could talk about the weather till the cows came home. He guessed it was about the only subject the two of them could discuss without an argument.

8

The shrill, tuneless voice rose in song, then cracked pitifully. A startled woodpecker, drilling in a nearby sycamore, fluttered away to a safe spot.

Where, oh, where is sweet, little Nellie?
'Way down yonder in the paw-paw patch!
Come on, Boys, and let's go find her,
'Way down yonder in the paw-paw patch!
Pick up a paw-paw, put it in her pocket!
'Way down yonder in the paw-paw patch . . .

"Do I sound more like a redbird or a meadowlark when I sing?"

"To tell the truth, Abe, you sound more like a crow," Albert laughed.

The singer looked regretful. "I know I can't carry a tune for sour apples, but I sure like to try. Come on and join in. What song do you like?"

"How about *Babes in the Woods*?"

"Oh, that's a good, sad one—let's try it."

Abe kept time by waving his hand. Next, he wanted to try a hymn. But before they could start, they were surprised by a loud cackle. An old man, with shoulder-length white hair, was standing in front of his cabin, laughing at them. It was Squire Fuson, the marrying squire. Albert had met him at many a wedding.

"Abe, your singing sure takes the rag off'n the bush," the man said as he pumped Abe's hand, laughing all the while. "It's worse than any jaybird I ever heard. You take my advice—stick to making speeches and leave the singing to this young sprout." He peered at Albert. "Who is this, by the way? Some of your kin?"

"Wish't he was," Abe smiled. "This here is Albert Long of Pokeberry Creek."

"Albert Long, Junior. Why, I didn't recognize you, boy, you've growed up so tall. How's your folks?"

They shook hands and exchanged news about their families. As they talked, they had to keep raising their voices to overcome the noise from the Squire's cabin where somebody was having an argument.

"Quit your jawing," the Squire called out. "A person can't hear hisself think. I'm trying to converse with Abe Lincoln and his friend."

Abe's name seemed to work magic. Men crowded to the cabin door, all shouting greetings and urging Abe to come inside.

"They got a little problem," Squire Fuson explained. "I wish you had time to take care of it."

Abe backed off hastily. "Sorry, I gotta get back to the store. Mr. Gentry will be looking for me." He started down the path. Albert was glad to see that Abe was looking out for himself at last.

"I'm sorry you can't stay," the Squire called after them. "This is a law matter. I told them to wait and take it down to Judge Pitcher, but they want it settled now."

Abe stopped dead. "A law matter?" His long nose twitched inquisitively.

Seeing that he had aroused some interest, Squire Fuson hurried to explain the matter.

"See that gray goose penned up over yonder?"

Several men came out of the cabin and began to add their comments.

"Shut up and let me tell it," ordered the Squire.

The problem was much like the colt case that

Abe had settled some months earlier. At that time two men had an argument about the ownership of a colt. From the crowd that gathered, Abe had selected a jury. He instructed them to listen carefully to the evidence, then vote for the side they thought was in the right.

"I served as a member of that jury," one man recalled proudly. "We voted, the way Abe told us to, on the pre— pre— what was that word, Abe?"

"Preponderance."

"Yes. On the *preponderance* of the evidence."

"Why don't you say it in plain English?" his friend grumbled.

Abe explained it again. If one side had even a half cent's worth of evidence more than the other side, that was preponderance, and that was the side they should vote for.

"Let's have another trial about this old gray goose, Abe."

Every man present wanted to serve on the jury.

Abe held them off. "Wait a little bit—let me think."

Ducking his head, he stepped through the cabin doorway. The Squire hastened to pull up a rocking chair for the guest of honor. The rest of the men crowded into the room. Determined not to miss a word, Albert worked his way forward and took his place, cross-legged, on the floor near Abe's chair.

110

Head bent, hand over his eyes, Abe sat still, thinking. Presently he raised his head and looking majestic as a judge, ordered the plaintiff and the defendant brought forward.

Nobody moved.

"The who, Abe? You mean, the goose?"

Squire Fuson made an impatient sound. "Of course, he don't mean the goose, you ninnies. He means the two fellows who are arguing about the goose. Ain't that right, Abe?"

"That's right." Abe explained that the plaintiff was the man who was doing the accusing, and the defendant was the one who was being accused. The goose was the property in dispute and, also, the evidence. It would be a witness, too, he said, if only it could talk.

Pushed forward by the Squire, the two men involved in the fuss glared at each other and began talking at the same time.

Abe picked up a stick from the hearth and rapped it sharply on the wood floor.

"Order! Order! One at a time or I'll throw this here case out of court. First, the plaintiff may speak."

The man began to tell his story, sounding very sorry for himself. He raised the gray goose from an egg, he said, and had witnesses to prove it. When she got nice and big and showed promise of becoming a good egg-layer, she wandered away to the other fellow's farm—the way geese will—and now the other fellow was claiming her. His voice droned on as he told his story, then repeated parts of it to make sure the judge understood.

Abe listened patiently. Finally he rapped the stick on the floor.

"Thank you, plaintiff. I believe I understand your side of it. Now, let's hear from the defendant."

The second man stepped up. "Your Honor," he began.

Your Honor. A flicker of a grin showed that Abe was mighty tickled. Albert spied Mr. Lincoln standing in a far corner, watching with interest, and he looked pleased too.

"Your Honor, this here goose has been hanging around my place for a month or so, mixing with my fowl, eating my corn and mash, sleeping in my pen. Now, I ask you—since the bird has grown fat off my generosity, ain't I the one that's entitled to her eggs?"

He, too, dragged out his story until at last "Judge" Lincoln was forced to rap the stick for silence.

"All the evidence is in," he said solemnly. "Now for the verdict."

"Pick the jury, Abe. I'll serve." Every man present held up his hand.

The judge shook his head. "I don't believe

we'll need a jury. This case can be settled by compromise."

Abe explained, "Compromise comes into it when there is evidence on both sides but a preponderance of evidence on neither side. Compromise is when each side gives in a little bit till both meet in the middle of the road. Nobody gets the whole hog, and nobody gets skinned.

"Both fellows have a claim in the goose," Abe declared. "One raised it from an egg. The other fed and fattened it on his own corn. Both should share in it.

"A month from now it will be Thanksgiving. At that time, this gray goose will be ready for the oven. I propose that on Thanksgiving Day, this goose be prepared for a feast with both men and their families to share in it." He turned to the men.

"Besides the good eating, fellows, she will give up enough goose fat to grease all your children's chests next winter."

A cheer went up for Judge Abraham Lincoln's wise decision.

Quietly, Albert slipped through the crowd.

"Mr. Lincoln—"

Tom Lincoln didn't hear the boy. Halfway out the door he was stopped by several men who slapped him on the back.

"Tom, you got a right to be proud of that son of yours."

"Yep, for my money, he's the smartest young feller in Indiana."

During the trial there had been a smile of pride on Mr. Lincoln's face. Now the smile had disappeared. In its place was a look of caution and uncertainty.

"Abe's time might be better spent," he told the men sharply.

Quickly he turned and left the cabin.

Everybody else was hanging around, waiting to congratulate Abe. Why not his own father?

"I don't understand it," Albert said to himself.

Yet, perhaps he did understand. In the back of his mind he could hear his own father saying, "Too much praise isn't good for a boy. There's such a thing as a person getting too big for his britches."

The front door crashed open, and two ugly young men plunged in.

"Where's Abe? We heard he was here."

Squire Fuson looked at them coldly. "Well, he ain't here," he lied.

"Where is he then?"

"Went south on a load of cobs, and the hogs ate him."

The two, who looked enough alike to be twins,

did not crack a smile at the joke. They looked around suspiciously.

"There he is. Hey, Abe, we got a bone to pick with you."

"Go ahead and pick it."

They glared at him. "We warned you and warned you, but you didn't heed us. Now we've sworn out a warrant for your arrest with Judge Pate, across the river in Kentucky."

"What's the charge?"

Abe knew very well what the charge was, the brothers said. He had been running a ferryboat across the Ohio River, from Indiana to Kentucky, without a license, and that was against the law. They had a license to do it, and they weren't going to have some newcomer cutting in on their business.

"The case will come up next Monday. Judge Pate says you be there."

Abe promised to show up.

"And bring all the money you can raise, 'cause you're going to pay a stiff fine or go to jail."

"Get along with you Dills," Squire Fuson said angrily. "Ain't nobody, Judge Pate included, going to make trouble for Abe."

They laughed unpleasantly.

"Abe Lincoln may be the biggest buck around

this lick, but nobody is bigger than the law," they said.

After they left, the squire asked anxiously, "Is it true what they say?"

Abe agreed, "No man is bigger than the law," but that was all he would say about the matter.

"Albert and I must be getting back to the store," he said. "We've fooled away the entire morning."

"Are you coming to the husking bee next week?" asked the Squire.

Abe shook his head. "I'm two days behind in my work already."

"Then stop for a minute and say hello to the womenfolks."

Back of the cabin, a group of women were getting ready for winter. Over bright fires they were trying out lard, melting tallow dips for candles and making soft soap. Albert's mother probably was busy with the same tasks. Tomorrow he and Pa would have to help her. Fall was so busy, no wonder folks couldn't spare their children to go to school. Spring was busy with the plowing and planting, summer with the weeding and picking. Albert's thoughts leaped to winter when a person might find time to work with his head instead of his hands.

"Abe Lincoln! What are you doing in these parts?"

116

He went among them talking and laughing, even taking a hand at stirring the soap kettle.

"Abe says he won't be able to come to the cornhusking," complained the Squire.

"It's just as well," one woman teased. "Abe always gets more than his share of red ears."

Albert scowled. He would rather attend a funeral than a husking bee. No matter how careful he was, he was sure to unwrap an ear of red corn now and then. That gave any girl present the right to rush over and kiss him on the cheek. The grown-ups always laughed, just the way they were laughing now.

"Here's somebody that might change your mind, Lincoln," the Squire bawled out.

Light as a deer, a young woman stepped from around the cabin. Brown hair curled softly around her face. Her eyes were as blue as chicory blossoms, and her skin was creamy as milk before it is skimmed.

"Howdy, Abe." She looked straight at him, then dropped her eyes shyly, and her bare toe drew a pattern in the dust.

At the sight of her, Abe turned into a different person. He hitched up his old jeans and tucked his ragged, paint-spattered shirttail in at the waist. Licking his fingers, he smoothed them over his unruly black hair.

"Howdy, Parthena."

Squire Fuson grinned as he watched them.

"Abe here says he won't be at the cornhusking a-Tuesday. Says he ain't got time. Don't you think he ought to take time?"

The girl raised her bright blue eyes. "It would be fine if he could come."

"Abe here says nobody will miss him anyway. You'll miss him, won't you, Parthena?"

"I might."

Abe's face grew bright. "How much will you miss me?" he asked, fishing for a compliment.

She flickered her long eyelashes up and down. "Oh, a bushel and a peck and a little in a gourd."

Squire Fuson dug his elbow into Albert's side. "Listen to that carrying-on. I recollect when Abe was skittish and shy with the gals. I'm glad to see him branching out."

Sure, the Squire was glad, Albert thought in disgust. All he ever thought about was marrying folks off.

At Parthena's answer, Abe vowed, "I'll come to that husking, if you promise to save all your red ears for me."

She giggled and covered her face with her hands.

What a bold thing to say. Albert was embarrassed for his friend and disappointed, too. It was all right to make the girl feel good, but there was no need to overdo it! Long ago he had discovered that all fellows Abe's age had this soft spot. But he certainly hadn't expected such behavior from a person who knew all about reading and writing and George Washington. Glumly, Albert sat down on a bench near the soap kettle and waited for Abe to quit polly-foxing around with the ladies.

9

Abe arrested! Albert would do anything, even risk Pa's anger, to help his friend.

"When do you expect to go to jail?"

"Next Monday, they said."

"How long do you reckon you'll be there?"

"Not more than a couple of hours."

"A couple of hours. Not weeks or months?"

Abe threw back his head and laughed. "Why, I'm not planning on being a prisoner. I'll just go up before Judge Pate, set forth my defense, and he'll decide in my favor."

Albert blew a big sigh of relief. "Oh, the judge is a friend of yours."

"Yes, he happens to be a friend," Abe admitted, "but that won't influence him. That isn't the way the law works. He'll favor me because I'm in the right—that's the way the law works."

He explained the troublesome matter:

"The Ohio River, between Indiana and Kentucky, has become a busy highway, crowded day and night with houseboats, flatboats, and passenger boats. Travellers wait on the Indiana shore to catch a ride downriver, but it's a lot of bother for the boats to slow down and steam in close to shore to pick them up. I can make good money by rowing folks and their baggage out to the boats. One day two fellows paid me a half-dollar apiece to row them out.

"So you see," Abe finished triumphantly, "I'm not breaking the law at all. I'm not rowing folks over to the Kentucky shore. I just take them halfway across!" His eyes shone. "I'm glad the Dill Brothers brought the matter up. Maybe Justice Pate will let me argue my own case like a real lawyer."

The river, with steamboats, flatboats, houseboats, and barges all on their way to adventure. Albert felt the old longing to go down and see them for himself. He wanted to hop aboard and ride as far as the river would carry him.

"Have you been as far as Cairo, Illinois?"

"Cairo! Albert, I been clear to New Orleans."

"You haven't!"

121

"Yessir. Gentry's son and I took a cargo-load down there on a flatboat last spring. Oh, the sights we saw! It's nothing like Indiana, Albert. There are Spanish ladies wearing silk and satin dresses and waving fans, and gentlemen with tall hats and gold-headed canes. Fine houses with iron balconies and great churches and every kind of ship at the docks and sailors from all over the world, speaking strange tongues.

"The streets are made of cobblestones. Every house has a courtyard and garden where red and purple flowers grow as big as plates and trees are hung with Spanish moss clear to the ground. The weather is warm and sunny all the time, just like June in Indiana."

Albert ached to see it for himself.

"Why didn't you stay then? Wouldn't you like to live in such a place forever?"

Abe looked grim. "I wouldn't, and you wouldn't either. They got other things that aren't so pretty down South. Things that Hoosiers aren't used to, like slavery. I'd heard about it, but I never realized what it was really like."

There were the whipping blocks and the slave markets where Negro families were separated and sold, one by one. Children were taken from their mothers' arms. Healthy, young colored men and women were pinched by their owners and trotted up

122

and down to show their strength, the way folks up north showed their work horses. Negroes, old and young, were chained, whipped, bought and sold like farm animals.

Now Albert knew what his father meant when he said that slavery was a disease that must not be allowed to spread into the free states like Indiana.

"It's bad," he said solemnly.

"Worse than you can imagine, Albert. If ever I get a chance to hit it, I'll hit it hard."

There was one real bad experience on the trip. One night Abe and young Gentry tied up along the sugar coast, near New Orleans, and went to sleep. About midnight a gang of Negroes with clubs climbed aboard, jumped the sleeping boatmen and tried to steal the cargo. A furious fight took place and Abe still had a scar on his forehead to prove it.

"That might have turned you against blacks forever!" Albert exclaimed.

Abe shrugged. "Why should it? This other scar is where a mean horse kicked me once, and I don't hold it against all horses. Those were mean Negroes that attacked us, but all black folks aren't alike, any more than all white folks.

"Anyway, we soon forgot the incident once young Gentry and I got aboard that steamboat. We left our old flatboat in New Orleans and rode home in style, like kings."

Albert sighed in envy. River life was the life for him. Abe said he once thought of running away from home to join a ship's crew.

"But a friend persuaded me that it was my duty to stay with my family till I was twenty-one. And I'm still here and not any farther along, because my father sure isn't interested in any more education for me."

"What is it that makes your father and mine so set against learning?" The answer took Albert by surprise.

"They're plain scared."

Scared? Albert thought of his father who would take down his gun and go out into the dark night to investigate strange sounds. He recalled Pa, white and shaky, nursing the whole family through the fever, though he had been as sick as the rest.

"My father ain't scared of nothing."

Abe repeated it. "Yes, they are. Scared of new times and new ways and new ideas. They're afraid of getting cheated like your daddy almost was by Peabody, like my father was once in Kentucky by a man who knew more than he did. They got a right to be frightened. A man without an education is as helpless as a fellow in the woods without a gun."

Abe had warmed up to his subject. You would

124

think he was addressing a whole crowd instead of just one boy.

"We got to have educated men with new ideas to keep this country going. Around here they say, 'What was good enough for my father and grandfather is good enough for me.' But there's no progress in thinking that way."

"Well, you're almost twenty-one now, so what holds you to your family?"

"Duty, Albert," he said mournfully. "Duty is a hard word. My mother says they can get along without me up in Illinois, but they depend on me a lot—always have, always will, I guess."

If Abe stuck by his folks, his future seemed plain enough to Albert. Rail-splitter, house-raiser, hog-killer, baby-sitter. They would keep him so busy working, he'd never have time to study or think.

"Doesn't a person have a duty to himself, Abe?"

"What do you mean?"

Albert didn't know exactly how to put it. "Doesn't a person owe it to himself and his country to be all that he's cut out to be?"

Abe gave him a long, thoughtful look. "Yes, I guess a fellow does, if he can get around to it. Still," he shook his head, "I reckon my first duty is to help my folks."

The idea of his friend's leaving Indiana made Albert feel panicky.

"Land sakes," he said crossly, "first, you say you won't go to Illinois with them, now you say you will. What does it take for you to decide?"

"Resolution. That's what it takes. Resolution is just about the most important word in *Webster's Dictionary*. It means making up your mind and sticking to it.

"Once I become resolute, I'm all right," Abe declared. "I walk slow but I never walk backwards. Oh, but it's hard to make up my mind what is the best thing."

Albert understood the word. He was resolute that he would do everything in his power to persuade his friend to stay in Indiana.

"Make up your mind to be somebody," he urged. "Stay right here and study law with the judges you know. Go up to Indianapolis and read the law books. Indiana is the place for you."

Most older folks would have told him to hold his tongue, but not Abe. He knew good advice when he heard it, even though it came from someone younger.

"You may be right," he nodded.

Albert felt so happy about persuading his friend to stay that he added generously, "Of course, if you could do your duty to yourself and your folks at the same time, it would be fine. But it don't hardly seem possible."

Again, his companion gave him one of those strange, thoughtful looks. They walked along silently, Abe frowning, pulling at his lower lip, thinking hard, as if the world had handed him all its problems, and he was the judge in the biggest court of all.

Within sight of Gentry's store, he turned to Albert.

"Thank you."

"What for?" the boy asked in surprise.

"Oh, for talking and listening to me with an open mind. You know, open minds aren't as plentiful around these parts as blackberries."

He began to fish in his pocket. "I want to give you something to remember me by."

It was a jackknife! Not a new one, but Albert would rather have owned it than any jackknife in the world. He reached for it eagerly, then drew back his hand.

"You shouldn't do that, Abe," he said cautiously. "You know that folks say it's bad luck to give a knife as a present. It's liable to cut a friendship in two."

Abe pressed the knife into his hand. "Take it for good luck. I pledge this knife to cut through nothing but difficulties for you."

Grinning, Albert accepted the gift. He gazed at it proudly, then stuck it in his pocket. Now he would give his rabbit's foot to his little sister. This jackknife was better luck than any old animal paw. All his life he would hang onto it, though he needed no souvenir to remind him of Abe Lincoln.

10

The first, heavily loaded wagon rumbled to a halt. The second followed close behind. Snorting and stamping, the workhorses waited impatiently to be unhitched and led to the water trough. All the able-bodied men pitched in to help unload.

"Abe! Abe Lincoln!" Mr. Gentry hustled into the store and out again. "Where in tarnation is that clerk of mine? Halloo, Abe—are you laid up somewheres with a book?"

Out of the woods and across the clearing a pair of long legs came sprinting. With one leap they were on top of the wagon, and Abe was tossing down bags of grain faster than the men could catch them.

"Say, your reading man can work like killing snakes when he wants to." Mr. Long paused to wipe his forehead.

Hoggy Jenks chuckled. "You know why Abe's so fired up to get that wagon unloaded? He's digging for the newspapers at the bottom."

The clerk jumped down with a bundle of newspapers under each arm.

"Come on, everybody. Abe's fixing to read the news."

A frown crossed his face as if he would have preferred having the papers all to himself. The crowd followed Abe into the store.

"Gather 'round," he said patiently.

He took his seat behind the counter, tilted his chair back, and began to scan the first page.

"What's new, Abe?"

"Hold off a little bit till I see."

They stood quietly as if waiting for a magician to perform some wonderful trick that they could admire, even if they didn't understand how it was done. Their faces were awed and respectful as they observed how quickly his eyes moved back and forth and up and down the printed page.

"Well, there are big doings in our state. The National Road is almost complete through Indianapolis. The government has bought up land for the Wabash-Erie Canal. And, looky here, we're going to have a railroad line at Shelbyville!"

His audience groaned. "Taxes, more taxes."

"More taxes," he agreed, "but more profit, too, when folks can get their grain to market faster."

One man declared that he was against railroads, national roads, and canals because they cost too much. Besides, they were contrary to nature. If a human had been meant to travel that fast, he would have been born with wheels.

"The river was good enough for my grandpa and my pa, and it's good enough for me," he said stubbornly.

Abe shook his head. "But it isn't good enough for folks who live far back from the river. They need other means of transportation. They can't move their loads through the woods on a flatboat."

The man shrugged. "Let them worry about that."

The clerk read a piece from the *Vincennes Western Sun*. Indiana's governor, Jim Ray, was predicting that Indianapolis would be a great railroad center with trains coming in from every place and going out in all directions.

The crowd hooted. The story only proved what they had suspected—the Governor was touched in the head.

131

"Now, Abe, you know such a thing will never come to pass. Railroads all across this country? That's a hairbrained scheme if ever there was one."

The wagoners were the angriest of all. They made their living hauling loads for other people. Railroads would put them out of business.

"There's no law that says you can't change jobs," Abe argued with them. "If wagoning winks out, you don't have to stay a poor wagoner. You can become a rich railroad man."

"Not me. My pa was a wagoner, and I'm a wagoner, and that I'll be to the end of my days. Anyway, railroads ain't ever going to make any headway in this country."

Albert had been leaning on the counter, chin in hand, listening intently. How carefully and thoughtfully Abe answered the questions. The men trusted his judgment. It would be easy for a fellow with Abe's powers to mislead folks. Lucky for his listeners, Abe was honest.

"I'll be honest, too, when I'm sitting in his place," Albert promised himself. Now that he had had a taste of learning, he never would be satisfied to have the news read to him. He wanted to read and reason things out for himself.

"What else is new, Abe?"

The clerk scanned the next newspaper. "There's going to be a fair up at Vincennes where

132

they'll show new kinds of seeds and fertilizers and tools."

"I know all about farming," one farmer grunted, "and the old, tried and true ways are best."

"Look at this," Abe exclaimed. "Tom Jefferson's library will be offered at public sale in Washington next week. The money will be used to pay his debts. I'd sure like to buy some of his books."

Storekeeper Gentry, hurrying by with his arms full of pumpkins and squash, reached out and gave Abe an impatient push.

"Get to work, Abe Lincoln, and maybe someday you'll have enough pennies to buy your own newspapers."

The clerk waved a hand, absentmindedly. "Be right there, Mr. Gentry. Just a second more."

"What else is new, Abe?"

"I see the Society of Friends have removed six hundred and fifty Negro slaves from South Carolina. Levi Coffin and family, up at Fountain City, Indiana, have given shelter to some one thousand colored folks who were escaping to freedom."

"How do you stand on the slavery question, Abe?" a voice called out. "Don't you think we ought to stay out of the fuss, Indiana being free, and all?"

Abe rubbed his chin. "Slavery is sure wrong, if anything is. We must keep it from spreading into new territories. If I had my way," he went on, "every slaveholder would do what Edward Coles did."

The name of Edward Coles, the former governor of Illinois, struck a spark. Everybody knew how he had moved from Virginia to the North and set his slaves free. He gave each Negro family 160 acres of land and offered them paid jobs while they were getting settled.

"I reckon Coles could afford to be so generous," one man muttered. "He was rich."

Abe said he reckoned that Mr. Coles felt that a person had no right to grow fat on the labor of others.

Some of the men, however, insisted that slaves were property and the government had no right to tell a man what to do with his own property. Some came right out and said that slavery was a good thing.

Abe raised his eyebrows. "If it is," he said, "it is the only good thing that a person ever wanted for others but not for himself."

Someday, he said, the whole nation would have to face the problem because the country couldn't hold together half-slave and half-free.

"What else is new, Abe? Any jobs?"

"Yes, good jobs. The government is looking for men to be postmasters. All a person has to do is sort the mail and collect postage from the receivers of letters."

One man raised his hand timidly. "Does a postmaster have to be able to read and write?"

"I'm afraid he does," Abe said in sympathy. "What else is new?"

"Chief Black Hawk is stirring up trouble again." The reader frowned. "He is threatening to move his people back across the Mississippi into this territory. Can't blame him. The white man did move in and steal the Indians' land."

"Abe!" Mr. Gentry puffed in from the back of the store, "How come that salt pork is still setting on the back stoop? I told you to bring it in and pack it."

Abe looked startled. "I plum forgot."

Albert's father looked down at his son. "Did you order the supplies while I was down at the road?"

Albert shook his head.

"Well, what did you do all that time?"

"I talked to Abe, Pa."

"Talked? Good land, you and that reading man are two of a kind."

"Thank you, Pa," Albert said gratefully.

His father stared at him. "I didn't mean it for a compliment."

Abe was folding up the newspapers. "Guess

that's all the reading for today, folks. I better get humping before Gentry fires me."

"Much obliged for the news, Abe."

Hoggy Jenks rose stiffly. "You've given us quite a bit to chew on. I reckon it will hold us till we see you again in the spring."

The clerk busied himself with the papers. He seemed to have something to say but hesitated.

"Some of you I've known since I came to Indiana as a boy of seven," he began slowly. "I hate to say good-bye, but I better do it right now. I won't be here come spring."

"Not here! Where in the world are you going?"

"Up to Illinois," he acted as if he could hardly believe it himself. "Yes, I'm moving on to the Sucker State."

"Now, Abe," Hoggy Jenks's fat face took on a pout, "you told us you weren't going with your family. You said you were going to stay right here in Pigeon Creek."

"I thought better of it," Abe said. "Just today a friend persuaded me that I ought to try to make something of myself."

Jenks warned, "You're going to turn into a rolling stone like your pa. Tom Lincoln moved from Kentucky to Indiana to get away from bad land titles and slavery. Now he's moving to Illinois to get away from worn-out land and the milksick.

You can't keep running away from trouble, Abe."

"I'm not running away. I'm running toward something. Fleeing forward, you might say."

His friends argued with him, trying in every way they knew to persuade him to stay.

"What's Illinois got that Indiana ain't got?"

"Free schools, for one thing."

"Indiana has schools."

"So the law says," Abe agreed, "but schoolmasters don't stay long in these parts. They can't live on goose feathers and bear grease. Folks around here don't support their schools—they don't even send their children."

"Does he think people in Illinois will be any different?" an old farmer asked softly.

"If they ain't different now, they will be after Abe gets there," Hoggy Jenks declared. "Whenever I go home with my head as full of ideas as a cat full of catnip, my missus says to me, 'I can see you been listening to Abe Lincoln again.'"

The crowd tried to talk the clerk into staying. Where would they get their news? Who would read the papers to them?

"There's a new schoolmaster coming," he told them sternly. "You folks get busy and send your children to school, and each family raise up its own reader."

Mr. Hall stepped forward, dragging Joe with

him. "I'm sending my boy to school," he said smugly. "Our family sets great store by education."

Hoggy Jenks's face fell. "I don't have any children," he said sadly, "but I have half a mind to attend school myself. Go ahead and laugh."

They did. The thought of old Hoggy sitting in the schoolroom amused everyone.

Jack, the former troublemaker, pressed forward to shake Abe's hand.

"Stay among your friends," he begged. "You got enough learning. A fellow can be too smart for his own good."

"Nobody ever can be too smart," Abe said. "Everybody needs all the education he can get."

The old farmer winked at the others. "When you say everybody, Abe, do you mean females, too?"

"Yes, women and girls should receive an education," said Abe.

"Well, when you say everybody, do you mean Negroes?"

"Yes, I certainly do."

They hooted at the idea. "If you give a Negro an education, how are you going to keep him a slave?"

"You aren't," Abe smiled.

"Better keep them ignorant then," one man declared. "What a person don't know won't hurt him."

Abe looked doubtful.

"Just today you saw a man here almost get hurt by a business paper he didn't understand. If a poor, uneducated colored man can become a slave today, what is to prevent a poor, uneducated white man from becoming a slave tomorrow?"

He was asking questions that nobody could answer.

"Abe Lincoln! Get to work!"

"Coming, Mr. Gentry."

The men crowded around to shake his hand. Mr. Long was the only one who did not go forward. He was dickering with Gentry for a few supplies on credit. The pained expression on his face told how he hated to be any more in debt to the storekeeper. As he turned away with his purchases, his eyes fell upon the boots. He gazed at them for a minute. Albert caught the sadness in his eyes, but it hardly registered. The boots didn't matter. Nothing mattered except Abe's announcement. All hope for school, for everything, was gone.

His father shook his arm. "Let's be on our way. We have a far piece to go."

"I want to tell him good-bye, Pa."

"Hurry up then. I aim to be home before dark. We been tarryhootin' around here long enough."

Albert looked up at the clerk.

"I thought you weren't going," he said accusingly. "You let on that you were going to stay right here."

"Why, Albert, you gave me good advice," Abe exclaimed warmly. "I saw a way to do my duty to my family and, to myself. I'm going to Illinois and help them get settled, then I'll be free."

Noticing the boy's sober face, he added, "Cheer up. We'll be seeing each other again."

Albert shook his head. "You'll never be back to Pigeon Creek."

"Then I'll see you in Vandalia or Indianapolis. We'll both be fine gentlemen in plug hats and white collars, carrying gold-headed canes."

Albert forced himself to smile. "Before you leave, will you speak to Pa about school for me?"

It was his last chance.

Abe laid a hand on his arm and looked into his eyes as if he knew exactly how the boy felt.

"No, I won't. Your pa has heard everything I have to say about schooling. He wouldn't take any more advice from me kindly."

Albert was desperate. "Then how will I ever get there?"

"You're so determined, I believe you will make it. Remember what you told me, 'The Lord helps those that help themselves.'"

Clenching his fists, Albert hid his disappointment. Looking at Abe's face, he knew begging wouldn't do any good. Abe had made up his mind. He was resolute.

"I'll see you in Vandalia then, or Indianapolis," he said coolly as if he didn't care a bit.

"That's the spirit." The clerk laughed. "Good luck, Albert Long."

"Good-bye, Abe Lincoln."

11

The sun was slipping down behind the woods toward the flat fields. The two walkers hurried along. To be caught in the woods after dark, even with a gun, wasn't a pleasant prospect. The sacks and bags they carried were heavy and awkward to manage. Before they reached their destination they would have to stop several times to rest and exchange burdens. They wouldn't make as good time as they had earlier in the day when they had come into Gentryville, empty-handed, fresh from sleep and full of hope. The journey homeward always seemed longer.

Strangely, on this trip the travellers talked more. To keep each other company and to make the hours and the miles go faster, they talked of people they had seen in town and things they had heard, but they carefully avoided troublesome subjects. There had been enough trouble. His father seemed calm, but Albert knew it wouldn't take much to stir him up, so he didn't mention the Peabody paper or school.

Nothing had gone right, Albert thought bitterly.

"It ain't fair," he said, then caught himself. "It *isn't* fair—isn't, isn't, isn't," he practiced.

"What did you say?" Pa turned his head.

"Oh, nothing."

"Well, what is it? Speak up."

Albert hated to tell. It would sound foolish.

"I was just practicing not saying ain't. Abe says it ain't, I mean, it isn't right."

Mr. Long snorted. "Oh, he do, do he? Well, I'll say it if I please. Tell your fine-haired friend to put that in his pipe and smoke it."

"Don't suppose I'll get a chance to tell him. He's leaving Indiana."

"Good riddance. And I wouldn't be surprised someday to see him sneaking back with his tail between his legs. That's what usually happens to these fellows with highfalutin' ideas. Sooner or later, they go out on a limb and somebody saws it off."

Impatiently, Mr. Long shifted the bag of meal in his arms.

"Oh, I knowed this was going to be a bad day with no luck in it," he groaned. "I felt it in my bones the minute that dog crossed my path. Then the flock of pigeons passed by me. They were bad luck warnings, and I should have heeded them."

"Abe says those are just superstitions," Albert spoke up. "Abe says folks mostly make their own luck."

The older man turned on him fiercely. "Abe says this and Abe says that. I'm about sick of what Abe says. What if he can read and write a little bit? I could read and write myself if I was a mind to. So you can shut up about Abe Lincoln. He ain't the smartest fellow in this part of Indiana."

"Some folks say he is, Pa."

"I say he ain't. Setting up there telling folks to support roads and railroads and canals and schools." Mr. Long's voice was filled with scorn. "Easy for him to talk. He ain't got nothing invested. Don't own nothing. Pays no taxes. Lives off his pa."

Albert changed his bag of groceries from one aching arm to the other.

"But wouldn't it be handy to have a road through here?" he sighed. "Then we wouldn't have to fetch and carry; we could bring a team and wagon through."

"Don't talk roads to me!" his father exclaimed. "I don't want nothing more to pay taxes on. Nobody else around here wants them neither."

Albert didn't know when to stop arguing. "Abe says folks around here are plain scared."

"Scared of what?"

"Of new ideas, new ways, new inventions, of anything they don't understand. Abe says they just stick their heads in the sand and say that times haven't changed, when the truth is they're changing every day, and folks got to change with them. Abe says—"

Mr. Long stopped dead in the path. Carefully, he set his sacks and bags at the foot of a hickory tree. He turned around to face his son, and his eyes were cold. Albert took one look at his father and knew he had gone too far. Pa was hopping mad.

"Scared, am I?" he said slowly. "Well, I guess I'm not scared of a young'un who has got too big for his britches." He took a step forward. "I guess I'm not too scared to jerk a knot in his tail."

The boy jumped back in alarm. "Pa! I wasn't aiming to be fresh. I was just telling you what Abe said."

Mr. Long threw up a hand. "Not another word.

Spare the rod, and spoil the child, the Good Book says, and it's certainly true. Now, sir, fetch me a good, stout stick."

Albert dropped his bundles. "No, Pa, no," he whimpered. "I'll be good. I won't speak all the rest of the way home."

"Fetch me a stick," his father commanded furiously. "I've tried being patient, tried to overlook your foolishness, but you had to keep on and on. Now you've broke your plate with me! This will hurt me more than you, but you're going to get licked for your own good. Now march and find me that stick."

Something inside Albert told him to run, and his feet were itching to go, but his head wouldn't let them. He couldn't run away and leave this thing unsettled. He had to try once more. For once in his life, he had to make Pa see something his way.

He began to search frantically along the path for the smallest, thinnest stick. He had a lot of trouble finding the right one. His father stood by, arms folded.

"Quit your stalling. That one there will do fine."

Albert began to pray hard. If the Lord was going to help him with Pa, He had better hurry, because time was running out. Reluctantly, Albert

146

picked up the piece of wood, wincing as in his imagination he already felt it on the seat of his pants. It was long and paddle-shaped, stripped of bark on one side, with a smooth, flat surface. He gave it a second look and hurriedly began to fish about in his pocket. He brought out something and passed it over the smooth, clean surface of the wood.

"Wait, Pa!"

"Wait nothing. The longer you wait, the more it will hurt."

His father grabbed the paddle in one hand and the boy in the other.

"Bend over!"

"Before you lick me, look at the wood, Pa."

"No use trying to get out of it."

As the paddle swung high, Mr. Long took an impatient glance at it. His hand stopped in midair. He looked at it again. His grip tightened on Albert's shoulder.

"Well, what is this? Speak up." He shook the boy. "What are these hen tracks supposed to mean?"

Albert twisted around to look up in his father's face, trying to smile, not to look scared.

"That's you, Pa. It's your name. 'Course it isn't writ real good. I was kinda in a hurry."

Mr. Long stared at the piece of wood, then at his son, then back at the wood. His eyes narrowed suspiciously.

"Are you trying to fool me out of your whipping? If you are, you're going to get it twice as bad."

"No, sir. I wouldn't do that. Honest, it says Albert Long. Abe showed me how."

Slowly, Mr. Long relaxed his grip. When the boy wriggled free, he didn't seem to notice. He was busy studying the signature. First he would hold the wood at arm's length and stare at it. Then he would bring it up close and squint at it. Moving across the path, he sat down heavily on a fallen log, still holding the stick in both hands and frowning as if he wasn't quite sure that he approved of it. Albert watched him anxiously. Presently the corners of Pa's mouth began to turn up.

"Why, it don't hardly look like me, do it?" he said in wonder.

Eagerly, Albert sat down beside him.

"I think it does, Pa. I think the letters look just like you—kinda tall and important."

"Pshaw." His father gave him a little push, laughing self-consciously. "Quit your soft-soaping me."

Turning the piece of wood, he examined it from every angle. "Yes, yes, now I see. It does

148

resemble the name that the clerk wrote out for me. Albert," he hesitated.

"Yes, Pa?"

"Do you reckon—? No, I don't suppose so. You can't teach an old dog new tricks, they say."

"What is it, Pa?"

"Do you suppose that you could teach me to do this?" He looked doubtful.

Albert's heart thumped. The danger of a whipping was definitely past.

"I could. I know I could. It isn't very hard. You'll be surprised how fast you'll catch on to it."

Falling on his hands and knees, he began to search the spongy ground among the leaves for another piece of wood. He found a nice piece of birch and quickly he stripped off the bark and carried the wood back.

"Here now." He brought the piece of charcoal out of his pocket.

Placing his hand over his father's, as Abe had done with him, he began to guide gently but firmly. At first the gnarled, brown fingers were so stiff, it seemed they wouldn't move at all. Presently they began to work.

"You're doing fine, Pa. Keep going."

Breathing heavily, Mr. Long gripped the charcoal so hard that his knuckles were white. Drops of sweat stood on his forehead.

"Oh, this is harder than chopping wood," he muttered. "I never knowed anything could be so hard."

Over and over they wrote the name. At last Mr. Long wanted to try it alone. When Albert took his hand away, he grasped the charcoal as if it were a live thing that might wiggle away from him.

"Quit looking over my shoulder," he ordered nervously. "Go about your business."

Albert wandered off to look for more wood, but he kept watching his father out of the corner of his eye. From time to time he saw the man stop, look at his writing and shake his head. The boy was afraid that he would grow discouraged and give up, but he did not. The pile of wood at his feet grew bigger. Finally he stopped and took a deep breath.

"Come here a second."

He held up a sample. "What do you think?"

He searched his son's face anxiously for the verdict.

Albert cocked his head, studying the sprawling signature. The writing was not as good as his own, he saw at once. This was a skill that young hands could pick up faster than old hands which had been trained for other work. Still, Mr. Long had copied every letter correctly, and each attempt was better than the one before it.

"Pa, that's awful good," he said honestly. "I

don't know as Abe himself could have done better, first tries."

You could teach an old dog new tricks. It just took a little longer. If older hands could learn new ways, perhaps older minds could learn new ideas. Albert studied his father thoughtfully as Mr. Long picked up a fresh piece of wood and started to write. He was glad now that he hadn't run away. Nothing must ever come between him and Pa, as it had come between Abe and Mr. Lincoln. Both of them were good people, but somewhere, maybe about the time Abe was Albert's age, they had taken different roads, so that now they couldn't even talk to each other about anything except the weather. Abe got along with his stepmother, and Albert could understand that. He loved his mother, too. But nothing would make up to him if he lost Pa, the way Abe had lost his father. A growing boy and his pa could have different opinions, even arguments, but that didn't mean they had to be enemies.

Mr. Long's graying head was bent low over his work. Without knowing quite why he did so, Albert laid a hand on his shoulder.

The sun slipped lower. A twilight breeze, with a taste of winter in it, stirred the trees and sent a shower of crisp leaves drifting down.

"Pa, we better be moving on."

"Hmm?"

151

"We better go, Pa. The sun is nearly down, and Pet isn't milked."

He gave his father's shoulder a little shake.

Mr. Long jerked his head up. He rubbed his eyes. "By gum! It's about suppertime, and here I sit in the woods, playing school. My head must be getting soft."

Rising stiffly, he brushed the bark off his jeans and picked up his bundles.

"Wait a minute." He stopped. "Pick up those sticks there and bring them along. Put a few in my sack. They ain't—" he hesitated, "they *isn't* much good, but we can always use them for kindling. Watch out now, you're rubbing off my writing."

He looked around. "What happened to your bird? Did you forget it back at the store?"

"I gave it to Abe, Pa."

Albert expected a scolding. It wasn't every day that a boy got a nice, fat, hen turkey. But his father said nothing. Albert glanced at the dusky sky where the evening star had already appeared.

"Maybe I can find us a couple of quail instead. They're quick to fix."

His father shook his head. "Never mind. Your ma will have something for us for supper." He sighed. "I expect she's looking for me to bring her something extra, and I haven't got even a piece of bacon. We thought we'd be coming home with our arms full, but we got fooled, didn't we?" He tried to smile. "Well, 'What can't be cured must be endured,' as they say." The smile faded. "Seems like I've fallen down on about everything I've tried this past year."

Albert had never heard him speak so before, had never seen him look so discouraged. His shoulders seemed more stooped, his face more heavily lined. This was far worse than seeing him angry. Albert ached to say something, do something to comfort his father, to make up to his mother for the bad news she must hear about the Peabody deal. If only he were older, bigger, stronger, smarter.

Suddenly he remembered the folded brown paper in his pocket.

"I got a present here for Ma." He brought it out and unfolded it. "It isn't much, but she'll like it."

"What is it?"

"It's a verse from the Bible."

"Can you read it?"

"Sure, Pa, I'm the one that wrote it down here."

"*You* wrote it! Well, read it off to me."

Albert took a deep breath. "It says, 'John 11:35, Jesus wept'."

His father stared at him as if he didn't know

him very well, as if he was someone else's boy. It was a minute before he spoke.

"Pull out my handkerchief from my back pocket," he ordered gruffly. "My hands are full."

Albert handed him the red bandanna. Mr. Long blew his nose loudly, then turned without a word and walked ahead down the path.

Disappointed, Albert tucked the paper back in his pocket. He had expected some compliment, but the way Pa acted, he couldn't tell if he was glad or mad. They had gone quite a way along the path before Mr. Long turned his head and said, "I'm glad you gave that turkey to Lincoln."

Home was coming closer. The dense, dark woods had fallen away, opening onto clearings where the late sun still lingered. Friendly wisps of smoke rose from chimneys, and the smell of fried chicken, wafting through chinks in cabins, teased hungry travellers and hurried them along. The wind, which had sighed through forest oak and sycamore, rattled a welcome home in the dry cornstalks of the fields. Up and over the little hill ahead, the road forked. It turned left to lead to the Long cabin, not more than a mile. It turned right to the Halls' and the Grigsbys' and to the weatherworn log house where church was held whenever a preacher came by.

Albert hurried to catch up with his father.

They climbed the hill together and paused to look down over Pokeberry Creek Valley. The view was familiar to Albert. All the golden summers and gray winters of his life he had lived here. He knew every knoll and hollow, every pasture lot and split rail fence.

"Down there is where the school's to be."

Arms full, Albert couldn't point, but he jerked his head in the direction of a thin column of smoke that rose from a cabin, half hidden by an orchard.

"Looks like the teacher has moved in already. It'll be pretty cold for him, come winter, if somebody doesn't daub those chinks."

"Who's he boarding with?"

"With the Grigsbys at first."

Mr. Long gave a snort. "Poor fellow. He'll be glad to move on, as poor a table as Mattie Grigsby sets. And the Grigsby kids are dumb as oxes. He'll have a pretty time learning them to read and write."

Pa had the superior air of a man who knew a good deal about education.

Albert kept his eyes straight ahead. "It's a good thing the teacher can't taste Ma's stewed chicken and noodles. We'd never get rid of him. Yes, he would be just an extra mouth to feed, and I don't know as we could manage it."

Mr. Long whirled around.

"Now what are you trying to say? That I'm not as good a provider as Reuben Grigsby? I vow, Albert Long, if my arms wasn't full, I'd— Oh, don't think I don't know what you're up to. Let me tell you that you're going to turn off here and go along to Grigsby's place now. You're going to tell that teacher that you're coming to his school. You tell him that you're coming every day for a month or so and that if he ain't learned you anything by that time, you're going to get jerked out. Understand?"

"Oh, yes, Pa," Albert could hardly speak. "Thank you, Pa."

"Thank you, Pa," his father mimicked. "Thank you for raising a boy that's too big for his britches. Well, what are you waiting for? Give me your bags. I suppose I'll have to carry the whole load home by myself. Keep your gun—you'll never be home before dark."

He squinted anxiously at the sky. "Won't be much moon tonight. Better find yourself a pine knot and borrow some fire from Grigsbys to light your way."

"Who will milk Pet?" Albert asked breathlessly. "Who'll cut the wood?"

"I'll have to milk Pet myself, of course. I'll have to cut the wood, too. That's what happens to a man when his son gets highfalutin' ideas. But

156

I'm not going to do your chores every night, so don't think you're going to have your nose stuck in a book all the time."

"No, Pa."

Albert was eager to be off, but he lingered, overcome by a warm feeling of thankfulness and a desire to reassure his father.

"We'll all learn together," he promised. "Just as soon as I get reading or writing or ciphering, I'll teach it to you and Ma and the girls. Then nobody can ever fool us. We can buy or sell, move or stay, as we please. We'll never need to be scared again."

As his father listened, a change came over him. He seemed to stand straighter, as if a heavy pack had been lifted from his back. His tired eyes took on a brighter look of belief and hope. But he only grunted, "Scared—pshaw! I ain't scared of man nor beast.

"And you can tell your teacher when he can't stand no more of Grigsby's victuals, he's to move over to our place for a spell. I sure hate to see a fellow go hungry even if he is a schoolteacher."

He turned to go, then stopped. "Albert," his voice was so tender, it didn't sound like Pa. "Albert, I want the best for you. I hope you ain't biting off more than you can chew."

"No, Pa."

The tall figure trudged down the hill and along the winding path, getting smaller and smaller until it was seen no more.

His father was a good man. A brave man who tried to protect his family from all dangers. A kind man who never licked his kids, except for their own good. A smart man, too, though he didn't have book learning. He was stubborn, but it was right for a person to hang onto his ideas and not be blown about like a willow by every gust of wind. He wasn't like the men that stuck their heads in the sand and wouldn't change. Once Pa saw that a new way was right, he would never turn his back on it.

Albert had to be honest with himself though. One reason he felt so soft toward Pa was that he had won out in their argument. The day would come, he knew, when he and his father would lock horns over another problem. Pa would be hard-headed, and he would be too old to knuckle under. Then he would have to strike out for himself, as Abe had.

It was coming. Inside, he could feel himself stretching and growing beyond his father's cabin and the boundaries of Pokeberry Creek.

Before he left them, he would finish up the harvest and the butchering. He would stock the woodpile to last all winter. He might even build a little porch on the cabin where his father could sit and survey his fields, where his mother could take her ease at sundown. It was his duty to do so, but beyond duty, he wanted to.

But that day was a long way off. Eagerly, his mind returned to the present. Reading, writing and arithmetic. Somewhere there was the key to success. This winter he would study his head off. Next spring, or the next, he would return to Gentryville, walk into the store and say: "I've come to pay you the money we owe you. Now, I'll take those boots, if you please, and another pair just like them for my father."

Albert followed the evening star down the hill. He was going to school. Wait till Joe Hall heard about it. Wait till Abe found out. He wondered where he would ever see Abe again. In Indianapolis? Vandalia? Washington?

Gray smoke, curling and twisting from the valley, grew lighter in color as it drifted upward. Pearl gray, almost white, it spread along the violet sky, shaping itself before his eyes into a mansion with pillars.

President Albert Long, Lawyer Abraham Lincoln of Illinois is calling to see you.

Why, show Mr. Lincoln in. I knew him back in Indiana when I was a boy.

Howdy, Abe, glad to see you. Well, Abe, I did get to school after all.

I see you did, Mr. President.

Abe, I've carried your jackknife all these years and it's never brought me anything but good luck.

I'm mighty pleased about that, Mr. President.

You can call me Albert.

He lifted his eyes. He had almost forgotten something. He had asked for help and had received it, just like the boy with the loaves and fishes in the Bible.

"Thank you, Lord," he said.

Fearfully, he looked around. Nobody near, thank goodness. Suppose someone had heard him. What would they think of a boy who talked out loud to the Lord like a preacher? Shaking his head, he began to run down the hill. The sweet, cool, evening air rushing past him cleared away the visions.

It was a long way from Pokeberry Creek, Indiana, to the big world outside, but once you had made up your mind, you were more than halfway there. He and Abe Lincoln had made that start. They were on their way to somewhere.